LOVE IS

LOVE IS

•

Carolyn Brown

AVALON BOOKS
NEW YORK

PRINTED IN THE UNITED STATES OF AMERICA
ON ACID-FREE PAPER
BY HADDON CRAFTSMEN, BLOOMSBURG, PENNSYLVANIA

With love to my husband, Charles.
Happy 33rd anniversary.

Chapter One

Amanda Creole Hawk heard footsteps coming down the hallway. It sounded like cowboy boots, but it wasn't her father because he'd already been in to see her that morning. So who was it? Her curiosity was piqued until she remembered she had to meet another new caretaker that day. Someone to keep her company and do whatever she needed since this horrible accident left her temporarily sightless. Someone who would probably upset her— and who would be gone by the end of the day just like the others. She'd already had five caretakers in five days.

The first one had a high squeaky voice and must have been weaned on one of those old Victrola needles. She talked non-stop, as if Creole needed the constant chatter of a voice to keep her from going stark raving mad. The woman lasted until mid-afternoon, when Creole told her quite emphatically to pick up her paycheck and go home.

The second was a bossy thing, telling Creole that she had to get out of the house and get some sun-shine on her face or she would wither up and die before the bandages came off her eyes. She lasted until lunch time.

The third and fourth didn't make it past the first hour. And yesterday's human wonder had been a reader. She loved the sound of her own voice doing all the different inflections as she read *Tom Sawyer* aloud. She made it through the day, but Creole swore that if the woman arrived in her room the next morning, she would upchuck.

Creole was twenty-three years old and she'd never liked for anyone to read to her. Not even when she was just a little girl. The best reader in the whole world couldn't keep her attention for more than five minutes. . . . not even the lady with multi-voices. And yet everyone expected her to sit quietly like a docile little puppy while she waited for her eyes to heal. Well, her birth certificate didn't come with a codicil about possessing bushel baskets of patience. That virtuous quality had never been a part of her lifestyle. The new woman her father was interviewing right now had better be more entertaining and inventive than her five predecessors, or else she'd be leaving by the same door she came in so fast, she'd wonder if she ever had a job in the first place.

Creole turned her head toward the squeak of the door as it opened. "Is that you, Daddy?" she asked, knowing full well it wasn't him.

"No, it's not," a masculine voice answered, with just a touch of laughter. Surely her father hadn't hired a man to attend to her needs.

"Who is it then?" she snapped.

"I'm your caretaker for the next five weeks," the man said. An anger boiled up from the pit of Creole's soul. Her father, Billy Hawk, had said just last night that it would take a saint to live with her, and that even a band of angels singing her favorite song while walking on a tightrope couldn't please her. He'd also informed her quite bluntly that he would hire just one more person to keep her company and see to whatever she needed, and if her contemptible attitude ran that person off, then she could grope around in the dark for the next five weeks. And he wasn't going to feel sorry for her one minute of the long, black experience.

"Who are you?" The tension was thick.

"My friends call me Parker. You may call me Mr. Parker," he said lightly.

"Well, Mr. Parker, you may leave. I won't have

a man taking care of me," she said icily. What on earth could her father be thinking?

"I don't think so," the man said. "Billy says you've already been mean to five women, and he can't spend every waking minute of every day with you. So I'm the man for the job. I understand you've already had breakfast this morning, so we'll get right into the day."

She was even more beautiful than when she was a little girl. She still wore her jet black hair long, framing her porcelain features like an expensive piece of artwork. But then, she'd always looked angelic with that creamy complexion, those haunting moss-green eyes, and all that gorgeous black hair. But with her hot temper and inflated ego, Creole Hawk was a far cry from anything ethereal. She'd had a haughty attitude when she was a child, and, evidently, from the way she sat there in her velvet recliner like royalty on a golden throne, it had grown right along with her. She'd always treated him as what he was—the hired hand's son. It didn't matter that his father was Billy Hawk's best friend as well as the foreman of the Hawk Ridge Ranch.

"And who is going to dress me?" she snapped.

"You have bandages on your eyes, not on your hands," he snapped right back at her. "I expect I can tell you if your socks don't match, but surely to goodness you can put on a T-shirt and a pair of jeans by yourself, Creole. You didn't break either arm or leg in the accident, so don't act like an invalid.''

''Don't you talk to me like that.'' She whipped her head around to the direction of his voice. ''You are hired to do just what I say, when I say, and how I say, so don't you dare talk to me like that.''

''I'm here to help you, not baby you,'' Parker said. ''Here are your jeans, a red T-shirt and a pair of cotton underpants, along with a bra.'' He flipped through the top drawer of her dresser after a quick trip to the closet, where there were enough clothes to supply a boutique. ''Can you find your way to the shower alone or do I need to lead you?''

''You need to take your smart-aleck attitude and get out!''

''No, ma'am.'' He wasn't riled one bit, but rather enjoyed the role reversal—even if it was fifteen years after the day she told him the same thing when they were eight and nine years old, and he'd come to visit his father over the Christmas holidays. Only that day, he'd taken his wounded pride back to the foreman's cabin and pouted all day. And until this very moment, he had not had occasion to speak to Amanda Creole Hawk again. He visited the ranch for his two weeks in the summer, every Christmas, and one other holiday throughout the year, conveniently at the same time she left the ranch to visit her mother in New Orleans. And that suited him just fine.

''I'll call Daddy.'' She fumbled with the cell phone at her fingertips beside the burgundy velvet recliner. ''You won't even be here long enough to dock my father for one hour's work,'' she said as she felt for the buttons and dialed the number.

Billy Hawk had been expecting the call for the past fifteen minutes. He knew she'd be infuriated that he'd hired a man and expect him to fire Parker immediately. But Billy only had one nerve left after the wreck, the recuperation in the hospital, the surgeons, and now all these women she wouldn't tolerate in her presence. And that one poor little nerve was frazzled beyond repair, so Creole would have to suck it up and accept the fact that she had a male companion for the next five weeks.

''Hello,'' he answered the phone, a grin playing at the corners of his thin mouth.

''Daddy, tell this arrogant man that he's fired,'' she demanded, flipping her long dark hair over her shoulder.

''No,'' Billy said. ''I told you last night you had one more chance. Parker is that chance, and like him or hate him, you're going to be in his presence for eight hours a day, maybe more, for the next five weeks. No weekends off. Five solid weeks, Creole.

Do you understand? I will not fire him, and I will not answer this phone every time he does something you don't like. Love him or hate him. I really don't care. But you will live with him, so make the best of it.''

She slammed the phone down on the cherry end table with such force that Parker had to rush to grab a crystal lamp before it fell and shattered into a thousand pieces. ''So what did he say?'' Parker asked, knowing full well what Billy told his only child.

''He said one more infraction and you're out of here,'' she lied, and he chuckled. ''Don't you believe me?'' She set her full mouth in a firm line, daring him to say a word.

''No, I don't,'' Parker said. ''I laid your clothes on the vanity in the bathroom. You should be able to tell the difference between the jeans and underpants by feel. Your towel and wash cloth are beside them. I think you can surely start your own water,'' he said.

''You're an overbearing, egotistical fool, aren't you?'' She stood up and felt her way along the back of the chair and the bed until she found the wall with the bathroom door.

''I'd say that's the pot calling the kettle black wouldn't you, Creole?'' Mercy, but she'd gotten tall since they were children. She must be all of five-feet-nine inches, and without those bandages on her eyes, she'd make any man turn for a second look. She wore a pair of pink baggy knit pajamas with cats printed all over them, and he thought she looked adorable.

That's all I need, he rebuked himself for looking at her in such an unprofessional manner. *To fall for the queen of all the sass in Oklahoma. She's always been stubborn and willful, and this is purely business. To have an opportunity like this is worth putting up with her sharp tongue for five weeks.*

She slammed the bathroom door with enough force to rattle the pictures on the walls of her bedroom. She continued to feel her way around the bathroom, stumping her toe on the scales, bumping her knee on the brass vanity stool, and pinching her finger in the drawer as she hunted for her shower cap. Finally, she found the shower and jerked the knob, adjusting the hot and cold water until it was the right temperature. She'd show him. She could take a shower by herself and dress herself, too, and by supper time she'd have him out of the house forever. This was one battle she fully intended to win.

She washed her face, being very careful not to get the bandages around her eyes wet. The nurse came every evening to change the gauze, and Creole lived in fear that something would go wrong, leaving her blind longer than six weeks. She still couldn't remember the accident, but her father said a semi truck lost control in front of her as she drove home from college for the weekend. Her little red Chevy S-10 truck was totaled. She'd been told how lucky she was so many times, she grew weary just thinking about it. Those nurses and doctors and even her father didn't have to wander around in darkness for six weeks, listening to women who wanted to read *Cinderella* and chauvinistic men put upon the earth to be big, mean and bossy. She stepped out of the shower and groped around until she found the vanity again, picking up her T-shirt and draping it around her before she realized it wasn't a towel.

After several attempts, she finally got her clothes on, and knew a moment of exhilaration that not once did she need to call for help from that crabby old man sitting in her room watching television. *Old man*, she thought as she racked the brush through her long hair. Just how old was this Mr. Parker? She sure didn't see her father hiring some good-looking hunk to spend all those hours with her. But then it didn't matter if Mr. Parker was bald, toothless and wore bifocals as thick as the bottom of Coke bottles. She would only be bothered by his presence for this one day. Maybe if she asked him to read something really risqué to her, he'd leave of his own volition.

Parker opened his notebook and began writing as he waited for her to take her shower and get dressed. Her bedroom was as big as his efficiency apartment in Denton, Texas. She had good taste. A four poster rice bed in beautiful cherry wood didn't begin to dwarf the room. A thick comforter of burgundy velvet and some shade of pink satin stitched in diagonal stripes matched the burgundy recliner in which she'd probably spent far too many hours. The carpet was the same pink as in the spread, and the dresser, chest of drawers, and entertainment system were all sister pieces to the bed. He finished his first entry concerning her anger over being left without sight, trying to be totally honest and not letting his own feelings enter into the document, and then plopped down into the recliner.

He'd figured on a bigger fight than what she put up, and if she knew for one minute who he really was, she would probably be more than just steaming. She'd be cussing mad. The last big war would be a Boy Scout wiener roast compared to what she'd do if she knew the hired hand's son was her companion for the next few weeks. He could still hear Billy's laughter when Parker had cornered him at the corral and told him he wanted the job of caring for Creole.

"She's always been a handful," Billy said rubbing his chin. "And age has just made her worse. She'll have her way if it harelips the devil himself." He shook his head. "If she knew you was even offering, Johnny." He wanted to say yes just to teach his daughter a well-deserved lesson after this past week of pure bedlam.

"When Mom and Dad divorced, and I left with Mom, I began going by the name Parker instead of Johnny. I haven't seen Creole since we were kids," he said. "She wouldn't have to know it's me." Parker smiled brightly. "I doubt if she even remembers the times when we were just kids on the ranch."

"Sure wouldn't be wise if she did." Billy laughed. "Now tell me just why is it you'd want to spend your summer vacation like this? Good lookin' young man like you should be somewhere with a beautiful blond on a sunny beach."

"I'm working on my master's degree in psychology, and I'm writing a thesis about the senses. When one is lost the others become more acute to make up for the loss. This would be firsthand opportunity for me," Parker explained. "I'll take care of Creole as long as you won't tell her why—or else she'll be even more uncooperative. And you get a free babysitter."

"Whew, can't beat a deal like that," Billy said.

"You're right as rain, boy. If that daughter of mine ever knew it was Johnny Rollin spending time with her to study her behavior . . ."

"Not her behavior," Parker said, shaking his head. "Her senses. I don't expect her behavior to be anything better than it was when we were kids."

"Good, because it ain't," Billy said. "Go on in there and take over the job, son. Goodness only knows you'll earn that thesis before the next five weeks are over. You'll probably be wishing you'd decided to do your research on the mind of the criminally insane before the time is finished."

"Isn't that the gospel truth?" he muttered as he aimed the remote toward the television set and pushed a button.

"Who are you talking to?" She stepped out into the room, confident of her ability to wrap her father around her little finger and get rid of this feeble old man who talked to himself.

"To myself." He laughed a deep baritone chuckle. "Go back in the bathroom and turn your shirt right side out. You've got it on backwards and inside out. Feel for the tag and the seams, Creole," he said.

She blushed scarlet. How dare he laugh at her. It was her first attempt since the accident to dress herself. First the nurses and then the women, even if they didn't do anything else right, had pampered her by dressing her each morning. He could be a little more supportive and show some respect. After all, he was just the hired help. He wasn't an angel with a golden halo and big white wings. She stomped back into the bathroom, slammed the door again in anger and jerked the shirt over the top of her head, forgetting all about the bandages on her eyes. She felt the tag and the seams, and carefully pulled the shirt back over her head.

''Much better,'' he said, barely looking up from his notebook. ''Now, what do you want to do today?''

''Do?'' she snapped. ''I want to . . .'' She felt for the back of her chair and sat down before she realized he was already sitting there. She'd scarcely landed in his lap before she was right back on her feet. ''What are you doing in my chair?'' she demanded, blushing for the second time in only a few minutes, and hating the second time even worse than the first. A red hot heat fanned up from her neck and engulfed her face with such force that it practically burned the bandages off her eyes, making her wish she'd been a little nicer to yesterday's woman.

She'd have to remember to be a little more considerate of the next person her father hired to take care of her. A slow snort became a chuckle and then a full-fledged roar. Parker wiped his light gray eyes with the back of his hand, and got the hiccups.

"Well, I'm so glad you found that funny," she snipped, turning her back to him and trying to will the heat of the blush from her face. "You could have at least told me where you were sitting. And that's *my* chair. Mine. Do you understand that? You can sit in the one beside the desk or on the floor, but please do not sit in my chair. And what do I want to do? I want to ride a horse, or drive to town, or hike through the woods with my boyfriend, or dive off the high diving board into the pool. But I can't because I'm blind until my eyes heal," she said, exasperated.

"Well, that's no reason to shrivel up and die in this room, Creole. Today we'll take a long walk around the ranch," he said. "Sit down in your chair, Princess Creole, and let this poor pauper tie your shoes. But don't enjoy it too much, because tomorrow morning, you'll be tying your own shoes," he told her.

A cold, calm dread replaced the heat of the blush. After the wreck, she was unconscious for hours, and then the panic of being totally blind when she awoke nearly pushed her over the edge of sanity. The doctor kept reassuring her it was just for a little while, until her eyes healed from all the glass they picked out of them. Then her father took her home, and she'd been in this room ever since.

Butterflies danced in her stomach and her mind reeled at the thought of actually going outside. She couldn't do it. She wouldn't. Not even if the stupid jerk tying her shoes laughed at her again. She flipped her hair back with clammy hands and tried to find an excuse, but none entered her mind.

"Ready?" he asked, taking her hand in his and pulling her to her feet.

"No, I'm not!" She set her mouth in that firm line he remembered from childhood.

"Afraid?"

"Of course not," she snipped. "I'm just not going outside today."

"Fear is natural," he said in a calming voice. "You can't see and you don't even know whether you can trust me. I promise I'm here to help you, Creole, not hinder. It's not a sin to be afraid, and the last time I checked, they don't banish you from heaven for it, either. So loop your arm through mine like this," he said, showing her how to hold on to him, "and we'll take a long hike."

He led her down the long hallway and through the foyer out onto the porch before she balked. "I can't," she whispered, her breathing shallow and her complexion whiter than usual.

"Yes, you can," he said firmly. "Now we've got four steps down and then we're in the yard."

"Mr. Parker, I'm afraid," she admitted, amazed at how easy the words were to say once she swallowed all that pride.

"I know." He patted her hand. "But we'll overcome that in these next few weeks, Creole. Just trust me."

Chapter Two

The soft Oklahoma breeze fanned her long black hair over her shoulder. She tilted her face toward the heat, loving the way the morning sun warmed her skin. She drew her knees up, wrapping her arms tightly around them, wondering just exactly what this Mr. Parker looked like. His arm was strong and muscular when she held onto him, and his step firm and true when he led her down a cattle trail and around the ranch last week.

She looked forward to his arrival each morning now, but she'd be banned to a back seat on a barbed wire fence in the devil's playground before she admitted that to anyone. She'd learned that very first day he wasn't there to pacify her whims or to entertain her, and she'd also learned that he hated to read aloud—which at least gave them a small island of common ground. He was intelligent. He liked the same country-western music she did, and they also shared similar food likes and dislikes. Chili was on the top of their likes and Brussels sprouts would always be at the bottom of the list.

"So what are you thinking about?" he asked when he finished taking notes about her progress this past week. She actually looked forward to getting out these days, and once Parker got past the tough shell, he found that Creole was highly intelligent. She even liked Garth Brooks. If she weren't who she was and if he wasn't doing this job just to help with his thesis, he might even consider asking her out to dinner sometime. But he was Johnny Rollin—the poor hired hand's son. And if she ever found out he just took the job to research a real live person for his thesis, she'd breathe fire and brimstone.

"I wasn't thinking," she said. "I was feeling."

He smiled, but she couldn't see the grin on his handsome face, or the way his gray eyes twinkled. It had taken a whole week, but she was finally beginning to use her other senses. He opened his notebook carefully so she wouldn't hear the rustle of paper.

"Feeling what?" he asked.

"Oh, the way the sun is warm on my face," she

said. "You know something, Mr. Parker? I've been out in the sun every day for most of my life. Never could tan worth a flip, but I've ridden, played, gone for a swim, but I always took the . . ." She stumbled for words to express the deep emotions in her heart.

"Took it for granted," he finished for her.

"Yes, I did," she nodded.

"Tell me more about the feel—not necessarily the feelings—but the actual feel of things, now that you can't see," he said.

"Why?" She perked up, hearing something like the crackle of paper. She drew her black eyelashes down and cocked her head to one side. Why would Mr. Parker have paper out here in the middle of the pasture? Surely it was the wind blowing through the trees, she thought, dismissing the idea of him carrying around paper when they went out for their walks.

"Oh, I just wondered. You said you were feeling, not thinking," he told her.

"Well, you'll think I'm crazy, but I'm obsessed with touching now," she said. "After we took our first walk last week, I went home and went through every drawer in my dresser, just touching all my things. Yesterday, I dumped a whole drawer in the middle of the floor and refolded every pair of pajamas I own, just so I could touch them. I was so excited when I got it all done, I danced a jig. Bumped into the bed and fell on it, laughing like a grade-school girl who just got her first kiss.''

He chuckled, writing as fast as he could, trying not to miss a single word or nuance. ''What did you do then?''

''I laid there, feeling the difference in velvet and satin. You know the comforter on the bed is made of both, and I never even noticed they were so very different,'' she said. ''Just like this grass.'' She pulled up a hunk from the earth and held it toward him, tickling his nose.

''Hey, you'll make me sneeze,'' he pushed her hand back.

''Didn't know you were that close,'' she giggled. ''Did I get you with the dirt or the grass?''

''Dirt,'' he said.

''Good. You deserve it after the way you acted that first day. I'll get even someday for real,'' she promised. ''I only ever knew one other person as determined and egotistical as you.''

''Oh, yeah? Who was that?''

''Johnny Rollin,'' she said, and he stopped writing and whipped around to face her. Surely she hadn't figured out his deception in just one week.

''Who?'' he asked cautiously.

''Johnny Rollin,'' she repeated. ''You wouldn't know him. He's Hank's son. Hank is our foreman.

It's a long story. Sure you want to hear it?''

Little shivers chased up Parker's backbone even though it was August and hotter than blue blazes in southern Oklahoma. ''I'd love to hear it.'' He struggled to keep his voice interested and lively.

''Well, my daddy, Billy Hawk and Hank Rollin went to school together all their lives, and were best friends as far back as they can remember. Hank went into the service, and my grandpa died the year they graduated from Allen High School. Daddy inherited Hawk Ridge, and after four years, Hank came home and Daddy hired him to be the foreman. So they've been together forever—except for those four years.''

''What's that got to do with this Johnny fellow?'' Parker asked carefully.

''I'm getting to it,'' she said. ''Hank met a woman while he was in the service. Her name was Martha, and he married her and brought her to the ranch. They had a son named Johnny. Then Daddy married my mother, Evangelina, from down in southern Louisiana. He says he went to look at a prize bull her father owned, forgot the bull and fell in love with her the minute he laid eyes on her.''

''Oh, I see, I think.'' Parker heaved an inward sigh of relief. She hadn't figured out that he was Johnny Rollin—not yet, anyway. And maybe if

she ever did, he would at least have his paper finished and be long gone before the storm hit.

"Anyway," she continued, "when we were just
little kids—I was four, so Johnny must have been
five—our mothers both decided they'd had enough
of a little backwater Oklahoma town like Allen.
Martha divorced Hank and moved somewhere in
Texas. I guess she went back to where she came
from. I remember her a little bit. She was so pretty,
and she had these funny gray eyes with almost no
color to them at all. Kinda like the sky on a rainy
day. I used to think she was part witch when she
looked at me, and down deep I was afraid of her.
And my mother went home for a visit right after
Martha disappeared with Johnny . . ."

He waited patiently for her to tell the story. He'd
heard his father curse Evangelina for leaving Billy
so many times through the years he couldn't begin
to count them all. Billy was just a hard-working
rancher. He wasn't some big hot shot senator like
her next husband, but Billy loved that woman.

She cleared her throat. "There was another man.
One she'd loved before Daddy, and they had this
big fight. Then before they could get back together,
she'd married Daddy." She stopped again. "So she
moved back to her home state and married him as
soon as the divorce was final."

"I see," he said. "And what about this Johnny
fellow?"

"Oh, yeah." She smiled brightly. "That's what the beginning of this monologue was about, wasn't it? Well, I hated him. I hated him so much! If he would have died, I would have danced a jig right on his grave—even if Daddy would have taken a hickory switch to me for doing it."

"Good grief, he must have been the devil reincarnated for you to hate him so much." Parker laughed.

"No. He wasn't even a bad kid." She shook her head. Creole didn't bother to conceal the envy. "But his momma loved him enough to take him with her when she left. And mine didn't want me, so I just hated that kid."

"Did you ever see him again?"

"Oh, but he came back a few times when we were little. Just to torment me even more. Hank loved him so much, and Daddy doted on him, always talking about Johnny this and Johnny that. He was going to grow up to be the president—or at least a king. In their eyes, he was probably perfect. When he came for his visits, I was as mean to him as I could be, and he always just looked at me like I was dirt. Of course, he never said so, but I knew it was out of pity because he had a full-time mother and I didn't," she said. "Anyway, you remind me of him sometimes."

"I don't pity you, Creole," he said thickly.

"Amen to that." She unfolded her knees, stretching her legs out lazily in the sun's rays. Her fingertips toyed with a sprig of dry grass, and she wondered what color it was. It felt brown. Green grass was more moist, and this was crunchy. It was that time of year in Oklahoma. Even the wettest summer couldn't survive the blistering hot August sun. Plants might be made to withstand heat, but precious few—except for cactus and yucca—could withstand scorch. Evidently scorch had arrived while she was laid up in her air-conditioned room, waiting for the bandages to come off and life to begin anew.

"So does this young man I remind you of still come around to visit?" Parker asked.

"Nope, not since we were about eight or nine. He quit coming when I was here. I was about as rude as I could be, so maybe that was the reason. Maybe he just wanted all the attention and decided to fix his visits while I was gone. I don't know. I hadn't even thought about it until we started talking about feeling. To be honest, I probably wouldn't like him any better as an adult than I did as a child."

The clock chimed twelve times just as Parker laid his pen down beside the papers strewn haphazardly on the desk in his bedroom. He pushed the chair back and stood up, stretching the kinks from all six feet of his muscular body. It had been a long, demanding week, but it had been profitable. The thesis was coming along beautifully, and the library research he'd done couldn't begin to compare with the real thing—in the form of one temporarily blinded Creole Hawk. A woman who would spit in his eye if she knew the true identity of Mr. Parker.

"Need something to drink?" His father eased the door open. "Saw the light peeping out under your door and thought you might like a glass of lemonade."

Hank Rollin stood six feet tall in his stocking feet. His eyes were brown, and his hair was still jet black and thick. A few crow's-feet wrinkles were settling around his eyes and the corners of his mouth, and for the first time, Parker wondered why his father never remarried. His mother married just a year after the divorce, and he had a pleasant relationship with Les, his stepfather, and he loved his thirteen-year-old half-sister, Tory, with a passion.

"Thanks." He downed half the lemonade before he came up for air. "Dad, why didn't you ever remarry?" he asked bluntly.

"Might someday, if I ever get you raised." His brown eyes twinkled. "Got to get one kid finished before I take on another."

"Surely you wouldn't be thinking of raising a

baby at your age? Someone in the picture?'' Parker's curiosity was piqued.

''What do you mean—my age? I'm only forty-eight. Lots of men don't even get started until now, much less have a twenty-four-year-old son. And to answer your question, I am seeing a rather nice lady off and on,'' Hank admitted. ''But you got a paper to do, and a price to pay for it so high it might not even be worth it,'' he laughed. ''How you and that spitfire girl gettin' on, anyway?''

''Fine, I guess,'' Parker said. ''She told me today I reminded her of the egotistical Johnny Rollin.''

Hank laughed. ''That's the funniest thing I've heard in a while. You with an ego and she's without one, I suppose. That girl thinks every cell in her body is gold-plated and that the only reason the sun rises in the morning is to shine on her. If I didn't love the little twerp so much, I'd spank her myself.'' He slapped his thigh and wiped his eyes with the red bandanna he pulled from the hip pocket of his jeans. ''I'm going to bed on that one, Johnny. You better get some sleep. Tomorrow you get to keep company with the Miss Priss herself.''

Parker laughed with him.

Creole laced her hands under her head, and if her eyes hadn't been bandaged, she would have stared at the ceiling. Tomorrow Kyle was coming to visit. He'd called earlier that day for the first time since she'd been home. But he had come to visit once in the hospital. He would have come more often but he was giving finals. Sounded like a feeble excuse to her even at the time, but not everyone was cut out to sit in a hospital room with a blind patient. And she had to admit she hadn't been a model patient, whining about the bandages, the food, the bed, the pillows, and everything else.

She could hardly wait for his arrival. She wanted a hug, a real one, not a fatherly one or even a quick one from Julia, the cook and housekeeper. She looked forward to reaching up and wrapping her arms around Kyle's neck, lacing her fingers in all that gorgeous blonde hair, and pulling his mouth down to hers for a nice, long kiss.

Kyle taught chemistry at East Central Oklahoma State University in Ada. He was ten years older than Creole, but that hadn't stopped her from falling in love with him. They'd dated for the past six months, and she was ready for him to propose. He'd been raised in Dallas, Texas, and thought Ada was barely big enough to live in—and he hated the ranch. Horses, grass, trees, hay—they all made him sneeze. So it was quite a sacrifice for him to actually say he was coming to visit tomorrow.

Perhaps he realized how close he'd come to losing her in the accident and was about to drop down on bended knee and ask her to marry him. She smiled into the darkness, and decided she would wear something especially nice tomorrow. No jeans or T-shirts. Maybe her black linen slacks, red silk shirt, and sandals.

Oh, no!

Her toenails hadn't been polished since the wreck, and Julia wouldn't arrive in time to help her out with that chore. She'd have to wear shoes after all. Kyle liked her nails and toenails done, and he'd be sure to notice if they weren't. She would show him how well she got around these days. Maybe if he'd taken his allergy medicine, she could even loop her arm in his and walk with him through the pasture, or at least out to the porch, where they could sit in the rocking chairs as they talked.

He could tell her all about the kids who failed the final exam, and she'd tell him about . . . What intelligent thing could she discuss with him? She hadn't done anything or seen anyone except Mr. Parker all week. She couldn't go on and on about Mr. Parker, or Kyle wouldn't stay fifteen minutes.

"Guess I'll just have to ask lots of questions and keep him talking," she said aloud. "If he really pops the magic question, it won't matter if we talk anyway. We can just sit on the porch and . . . Oh, what a wonderful feeling to think about touching

his face and just entwining my fingers in his hand.''
She sighed and tried to will herself to sleep.

But it didn't work.

She counted fluffy, woolly sheep jumping over
white picket fences. She did the multiplication tables
through ten and then did them backwards, and recited
the first lines of ''The Raven'' so many times she got
bored enough to cry. But she still couldn't sleep. She
heard the clock in the living room chime three times,
sat up, and fluffed her pillow for the third time.

Her stomach growled. She longed for one of the
chocolate-chip cookies Julia baked that morning.
But the cookies were all the way down a long hall,
across the living room, through the formal dining
room and into the kitchen. There was no way she
could make it that far in the dark!

''But I have,'' she told herself when her stomach
grumbled again. ''Lots of times, I've raided the refrigerator without turning on a single light.''

She crawled out of bed, felt her way along the
wall to the door, and eased down the hall, using
the palm of her hand to guide her, being careful
not to knock any of the pictures of herself off the
wall. Six long strides into the living room and she
found the back of the long, leather sofa. Strange, it
was cold in the middle of the night with the air-
conditioning unit blowing down on it. She turned
to her right and groped around until she bumped

into the bookcase. A couple of steps and a sharp turn and she was in the dining room.

"One, two, three," she whispered, and sure enough, there was the table. Another right and she found the bar separating the dining room from the kitchen. And there, on the end of the counter top was the cookie jar. She recalled the yellow flowers painted on its side. She took the top off and slipped her hand inside to find it still practically full of nice, crispy cookies.

"Mr. Parker better watch out now," she giggled under her breath. "If I can find my way to food, then his job security is slipping."

She bit into the cookie. It had never tasted this good before, but then, she'd never had to work so hard for a midnight snack. Milk. That's what she needed to go with it! She fumbled along the cabinets until she opened the door with glasses behind it, and then she opened the refrigerator.

"Top shelf, on the left." She guided her hand cautiously. Suppose she sat caught? What would, Billy Hawk think if he woke up and found her? He'd give her a sound dressing down for being up at this ridiculous hour, groping around in the dark. Why, she could hurt herself by acting so irresponsibly.

She giggled again as she thought about her father underestimating the strength of a woman. She slipped her forefinger along the edge of the glass, and poured the milk until she felt the liquid on her finger. Then she picked up the glass, tilting it back. It was wonderful—she hadn't even spilled a drop on the counter top.

Yes siree, Mr. Parker would do well to watch his high-handed attitude. She could take care of herself for the next four weeks without a babysitter. She finished her snack, and reversed her tracks until she was back in her room between the covers of her bed. She felt immensely happy, and within minutes she was asleep, dreaming about Kyle with his cute round face and blond curls and shivering delightfully at the way her heart pounded when he held her in his arms.

But there was something strange about his eyes. They weren't dark brown with sparkling yellow highlights anymore. They were the color of the sky on a rainy day—just like the eye color Johnny Rollin inherited from his strange mother. She frowned in her sleep and willed herself to wake up. She didn't want to look at those haunting eyes—not even if it meant putting an end to her dream about Kyle.

Chapter Three

"So tell me about this Kyle fellow. He doesn't look like Creole's type." Parker picked up a warm chocolate-chip cookie from the platter and popped it into his mouth.

"What did you think she'd fall for?" Julia smiled brightly. The lady who kept house for Billy Hawk looked exactly the same as she did when Parker was just a little boy—running in and out of the house and begging her for cookies—and fighting with Creole. She was barely five feet tall, wore her black hair in two thick braids wrapped around her head, and could be anywhere from forty to sixty years old. No one had the courage to ask how far from or how near sixty the figure really was.

"Oh, I don't know." Parker grabbed another

cookie. "Someone taller than that fellow and maybe with dark hair. I never pictured her with a blond—especially one who looks like he only needs to shave once a month."

"You mean you thought she'd be with someone like you?" Julia asked bluntly.

"Oh, no!" Parker shook his head. "Just not someone like him. They been dating long?"

"Six months. He's older than she is, you know—by about ten years." Julia scraped more dough from a teaspoon, letting it hit the cookie sheet in a gob that didn't look like it'd ever flatten out into a cookie.

"Well, he must make her feel good," Parker said. "She was all fidgety today. I couldn't get her to sit still for more than five minutes and talk about anything. She told me this morning he'd be here right after lunch and I could take the entire afternoon off."

"She hasn't figured out who you are yet?" Julia asked.

"Nope. I thought she had a few days ago, when she started talking about Johnny. I held my breath until I thought I'd smother to death," Parker said.

"It's a bit of a mean trick, you know," Julia chastised. "Is it really worth all you have to endure to get the information you want?"

"Sure is," Parker nodded. "She's not so bad

really. A bit high tempered, but then that's just the Cajun and Indian blood mixed up together. Anybody who ever knew her mother and knows Billy Hawk couldn't expect her to be a mild-tempered lass who never spoke her mind, now could they?''

''I don't think so.'' Julia laughed, nodding toward the living room where they both heard someone stomping across the hardwood floor. ''Sounds like your whole afternoon off lasted about fifteen minutes. I suppose you ought to give her a couple of minutes, then go on back to her room and see what . . . Well, there he goes.'' she nodded as she looked out the window. ''He just lost about fifty miles of rubber off them tires spinning out like that. Looks like they just had a big fight. You might want to take the afternoon off after all. I'll go see if she wants to talk.''

''I'll go.'' He finished the last sip of coffee in his mug as he stood up. ''Fine cookies, Miss Julia. You haven't lost your touch.''

''Get on with you. And remember she's going to be mad, so don't go in there expecting that little damsel in distress you were just talking about her not being,'' she said.

''Yes, ma'am,'' he saluted smartly. When he eased open the door to her room, she spun around. The look on her face let him know that Julia hadn't misjudged the situation.

"Hello?" he said.

"Go away," she snapped. "I told you to take the afternoon off, and I meant it." She whipped back around to touch the silk drapes, rubbing them with her forefinger and thumb as she attempted to sort through the gamut of emotions running rampant inside her heart and head.

"Think I'll stay." He sat down in her recliner and fumbled with the remote until he found the CMT station they both liked. "I'm in your chair, so don't back up and sit in my lap," he cautioned her calmly.

She didn't say a word, although a million words were running through her mind. She might call that petty creep on the phone later and unleash about half of them into his ears, or she might collect them all into a bin and bury them forever and just never speak to him again. One thing for sure, she was through trusting anyone. Every time she thought she loved someone, they went away. She was tired of the pain.

She could hardly wait for Kyle to get here today. She made Mr. Parker tell her a dozen times that her slacks weren't wrinkled, that her hair was combed perfectly, that her lipstick wasn't smeared. Her heart did flip-flops when she heard the gravel crunch under the tires of his little black sports car as he drove up the circular driveway outside.

Creole heard Parker sneeze, so she made a mental note not to ask him to go for a walk with her or to sit on the front porch in the swing. He could sit in her recliner and she'd sit nearby.

"Creole?" Kyle said as he opened the door, and she turned to face him. Even though she couldn't see him, she could visualize the smile on his face. She waited for him to cross the room, take her in his arms and tilt her head back for a long, passionate kiss.

"Kyle, I'm so glad you came." She couldn't contain her excitement.

"I can't stay long," he said bluntly. "I've come to talk to you."

"Sit down, and I'll sit beside you." She motioned toward the chair, realizing now that she looked back that his tone should have told her what he was about to say.

"No, I'm not staying that long," he said. "I don't know how to say this other than to just spit it out. This is not working, Creole. I'm not going to see you again. I thought about calling and telling you on the phone, but that seemed to be a childish way out."

"Why?"

"Because I don't love you," he said. "You're not my type, Creole. You're young and vivacious and fun to be with, but I could never spend a lifetime with you. And I'm ready to settle down to a house, a wife and kids.''

''Why couldn't you spend a lifetime with me?''

''Because I don't want to. I've found someone else. She makes me feel like I'm the king of the world. And—''

''Then you better take your sorry old hide out that door and get on back to her,'' Creole told him. ''Who is she, anyway? And didn't I make you feel like that?''

''No, you didn't,'' Kyle said defensively. ''You make anyone you're with feel like they're lucky just to be in your presence. You might do well to work on your attitude if you want someone to really fall in love with you,'' he said.

''I don't think I need a lecture today,'' she told him coldly, wishing she could put even more icicles in her tone.

''Good-bye, Creole,'' he told her. ''It's been fun these past few months. I wish you all the best.''

''Oh, sure you do,'' she snorted. ''Just go away, Kyle. And when your new friend breaks your little heart, don't come back here expecting me to step back into your life.''

On the television, Travis Tritt was singing something about a broken heart. Things should be shattering in her heart, but strange as it was, her heart wasn't really hurting. It felt numb. She listened intently to Parker breathing. She knew he was staring at her rather than the television. How strange. She could actually hear which way his head was turned.

"What are you looking at?" she snapped at him.

"The television," he chuckled.

"No, you weren't. I could hear you breathing," she told him.

Parker's eyes widened and he took the tiny notebook from his shirt pocket, flipped it open and wrote down what she'd just said. Her sense of hearing was intensifying, and she was as aware of it as she had been several days ago when she found she could actually see with her fingertips.

"Oh, you did?" he teased. "Tell me what else you hear?"

"I hear a fifty-five gallon drum of anger about to explode inside of me," she said honestly.

"What does it sound like?"

"It sounds like anger. Pure old rage. I've wasted six months of my life on Kyle, and now he tells me he's found someone who makes him feel like a king," she spit out vehemently.

Parker could relate to the fair-haired man with crow's feet wrinkles around his blue eyes. That's just the effect Creole had on men. She was the queen and they were just chattel. Kyle was wise to see that he didn't have the stamina to tame so great a force.

And yet to tame it wasn't what a man should do either, he reasoned with himself. To harness all that energy and beauty into a permanent relationship would be the hardest thing a man ever did, but also the most rewarding. Because under that shell of beauty lay a potential lifetime of dynamite. Whoever married Creole would never live a ho-hum life of doldrums. They'd never have a boring day. They'd wake each morning to a new emotional roller-coaster. There would never be a dull moment.

"You're not going to weep and wring your hands around a lace hanky like the poor discarded southern belles in the movies, are you?" he continued to tease.

She snorted.

"You're not going to grope your way through the front door and fall in the gravel where his tire marks are and sling mud?"

She giggled.

"You're not even going to make me drive you to his house and beg him to let you serve him as king?"

She roared in laughter until she got the hiccups.

"Get out of my chair," she demanded. He stood up and allowed her room to flop down. "I've always handled everything with anger," she said. "When Momma left me behind and married my stepfather, I pitched such a tantrum that Julia threatened to take me to the woodshed if I didn't straighten up. Daddy might have let her, too. And ever since then, I've handled my upsets with anger, not tears. I don't cry. I get even and Kyle better watch out because I'm really, really mad.''

''Want to go for a walk?'' Parker asked.

''Sounds wonderful,'' she said. ''Take me out to the pond and let me sit where I can hear the frogs. Maybe they'll take part of this mad spell away.''

''Did he even hug you or kiss you before he pronounced the judgment?'' Parker asked.

''That's none of your business.'' She reached for his arm, looping hers through it like she'd done so many times.

''Sorry sucker,'' Parker whispered. ''He's not too bright. Don't waste all that good anger on him. You might need it later for someone else and then it will be all gone.''

''Oh, hush,'' she hiccuped again. ''I knew down deep in my heart he was drawing away. I just didn't want to face it. Please get me out of this house, or I might unleash all that anger on you, Mr. Parker.''

''Yes, ma'am.'' He snapped the heels of his cowboy boots in a loud popping noise. ''I surely do not want to be on the receiving end of such a fit.''

* * *

Creole drew her knees up and wrapped her arms around them, like she did when she was deep in thought. Parker watched her, staring as long and boldly as he wished. Kyle might have been wise in one way, but he was a fool in another because Creole Hawk would make some man a wonderful partner to accompany through the journey of this life. She was as blunt and honest as Billy Hawk, as beautiful as her mother, as wild as the wind. He hoped that when he decided to settle down and find a wife that he could find someone who would stir his passions like she could.

Oh, no, he argued with that voice inside his head. *Creole is just a subject for research. I'm digging deep into her emotions and heart, but what I put on the paper is as far as it goes. I do not intend to take even one little portion of that woman off the thesis and into my own life, and that's a fact.*

"Mr. Parker, dance with me," she said suddenly.

"But Creole, we have no music," he protested.

"Listen to the wind, the way it flows through the leaves on the trees. I hear the frogs as they sing their love songs. Listen to the storm cloud off in the southwest." She nodded in that direction, and he was amazed to see a black bank of clouds pushing toward them.

"Did you hear all those things when you were

able to see?'' He stood up and pulled her to her
feet.

''No, I didn't. And I didn't feel the difference in
velvet and satin. And I didn't see my heart or my
emotions for what they are, either. I just went
through life, like everyone else. A day at a time,
taking everything for granted, and pushing my way
through every experience. But not today. Today I
am sad, Mr. Parker. I'm sad because I wanted Kyle
to hug me. I wanted to feel his arms around me,
and instead he just made me as mad as a wet hen
in a rainstorm. So hum a tune and dance with me.''
She raised her arm, searching for his shoulder.

He touched her hand, guiding it toward his neck.
''I hum off-key,'' he admitted. ''Never could sing
or hum a tune without a bucket to carry it in.''

''Then I'll hum.'' She took a step closer and
melted into his arms.

There in the middle of the pasture Creole began
to sing a beautiful Cajun ballad her mother taught
her years before, when she was just a little girl.
The storm approaching Allen, Oklahoma from the
southwest was just a gentle breeze compared to the
hurricane twisting inside Parker's heart. He hoped
that when she laid her head on his chest that she
couldn't hear the double time beat of his heart, and
that she didn't know the effect she had on him as
she sang in the clear, sweet voice of a young girl

on the bayou waiting forever for her lost love to return.

Late that night, Creole snuggled down into the sheets, listening intently to the thunder and the driving rain as it beat against the glass doors leading from her bedroom to the deck at the back of the house. It sounded ominous and threatening, just like the anger she'd felt this morning when Kyle told her he was in love with someone else. But she was safe and warm—just like in Mr. Parker's arms this afternoon.

Oh, no. She shook her head violently. *Don't entertain such an idea. He was there, but he's hired help, not someone I could ever be interested in starting a relationship with. He was nice to dance with, nice to hold, and he might even be a nice fellow. But Mr. Parker is not for me. Even though he feels solid and his voice sounds young, he's probably old and bald, and maybe even wears dentures. So don't you go building him up in your blind eyes to be a knight in shining armor, Creole Hawk. Just shut your mind off and go to sleep to the rhythm of the falling rain.*

"Oh, sure," she said aloud. "Go to sleep when all I can think about is the way his heart raced when I insisted he dance with me."

Chapter Four

Parker grabbed a biscuit, stuffed a sausage patty inside, and rolled his eyes in appreciation when he bit into it. "Did you make these or did they come straight from Heaven?" he asked.

"Get on with you." Julia smiled brightly, her dark eyes dancing. "You always was a charmer, Johnny Rollin, even as a child."

"Shhhh." He touched his lips with his forefinger. "Mr. Parker, not Johnny Rollin. We don't want to mess up the assignment right here in the middle of the job, Julia."

"Nope, we sure don't." She shook her head seriously. "She's almost bearable these days. If we had to hire another person, she'd go back to acting like a grizzly with an ingrown toenail."

He patted her on the shoulder and made his way back down the hallway to Creole's room. "Good morning," he called after a brief knock on the door. "Well, well, progress abounds. You've already had your shower and gotten dressed. I'm impressed, Creole. Let me see." He studied her closely, enjoying the moment more than he wanted to admit. "Socks match, shirt on right side out, jeans zipped up in the front instead of the back . . ."

"Hush!" she snapped good-naturedly, enjoying the bubbly feeling in her heart as he teased her. "I'm blind, not deaf, not dumb. And I can dress myself, thank you very much!"

"Just kidding," he chuckled.

"Do we finally have a cool morning to take a walk, or is it still blistering hot?" Creole asked. "That little rainstorm we had last week sure didn't lower the temperature much, did it?"

"Nope, but it's a wonderful morning, and I've got something nice in store. Today we're going out," he told her.

"Okay." She fumbled with the remote until she found the right button to switch off the television and then stood up. "You get the blanket . . ."

"Already did. It's in my truck," he said.

"Why?"

"Because we're going for a drive. Wherever you want, and then wherever I want. A compromise," he told her. "You need to shop for anything? We'll go to the department stores. But lunch and the rest of the afternoon is up to me. I have a surprise."

The palms of her hands were clammy with dread. Her heart felt as heavy as a chuck of solid concrete. She held her breath until the room began to sway and she thought she'd faint. She couldn't get into a truck and go somewhere with him. What if they had a wreck? What if he was unconscious? She couldn't see to find help or to even help herself. She sat back down in her recliner, wishing she could pull the velvet sides around her like a blanket and wrap up in her own safe little world until the bandages came off in two weeks. Of course, Mr. Parker was only interested in her well-being. He probably thought she'd be elated to leave the ranch for a day. But even when she had the bandages off and could drive again, she would still get the shakes just thinking about crawling inside a pickup truck again.

Suddenly a Technicolor vision of a truck swerving all over the road in front of her was burned into the blackness behind her bandages. No matter how hard she stomped the brakes or gripped the steering wheel, she knew she would hit the truck. And then there was nothing but darkness followed by a bright white light and someone peering down into her face. Someone who smelled like the bathroom after Julia scrubbed it with disinfectant.

"Creole?" Mr. Parker sounded concerned. But he wasn't the one who wiped the blood from her face.

"A cut above the left eyebrow and glass in both her eyes," the feminine voice had said. So there had been at least one woman doctor in the emergency room that night. Why was she remembering the whole affair this morning? And what on earth triggered the memory?

"I cannot go," she whispered hoarsely. It was the fear. The same heart-stopping fright she felt that day when she knew beyond a shadow of a doubt she was going to collide with the side of that truck. And she could not make her jelly-filled knees stand up and support her, let alone carry her all the way down the long hall across the living room to the porch. She would not remember to breathe if she did make it to the yard where his truck must be parked. And her heart would go into an acute cardiac arrest at the ripe old age of twenty-three if she actually belted herself into a truck. The last time she rode in a vehicle was when her father rode beside her in the ambulance to bring her home. She refused to ride in his truck that day, so Hank rode to the hospital with Billy and drove the truck back to Hawk Ridge.

"Creole?" Mr. Parker asked again, sincere concern in his voice.

"I will not go anywhere except for a walk around the ranch . . . just like we do every day," she yelled, wondering where all the volume came from since she could scarcely breath.

"Okay," he said. "Then let's go for a walk."

Her heart resumed its normal beating pattern and the keg of dynamite she felt like she was sitting on disappeared. She'd finally won a round with this obstinate man her father had found under some obscure rock. Well, would wonders never cease? All she had to do was shout a little and he backed right down. She must remember that in the future. She stood up slowly, expecting a rush but nothing happened.

"Take my arm, Lady Creole." He took her hand. "We shall go outside and feel the sunshine on our faces and talk about all the wonderful things which have happened since last night when the moon rose in the sky. See there, I can be very poetic. Would you like for me to pick up a copy of Shakespeare or Elizabeth Barrett Browning as we stroll through the living room? Perhaps you would like to listen to the frogs and crickets sing while I read poetry or *Romeo and Juliet* to you this fine morning." He held back his laughter.

"Sarcasm will get you nowhere," she snipped.

"I thought that was flattery," he said, smoothing the edges of her temper.

"That, too," she told him. "If you start reading to me, I'll fire you on the spot, even if I have to listen to the voices on television for the next two weeks."

"Yes, ma'am. Whatever you say, ma'am. Shall I kiss your toes now, or will you have me wait with my face in the dirt until you give the command?" he chuckled.

"I mean it." She set her mouth in a firm line that left no doubt that he was walking on very thin ice. Well, Creole Hawk didn't know it, but it was about to get even thinner in the next few minutes, and if he fell into the icy water of her wrath, so be it. He wasn't going to let his plans for the day be thwarted. Besides she would probably enjoy all he'd arranged for her pleasure before the sun set tonight.

"We are at the edge of the porch. Four steps down and then the yard," he said, seriousness returning to his voice. "Now we're across the yard, and here is my truck. I'm opening the door and you have a choice. You can either crawl up in the seat, or else I will pick you up and put you in it, because today we are leaving the ranch, Creole. I know you are terrified to ride in a truck again, and I understand that. But like I told you that first day, you can trust me. I'm not going to leave you.''

"Take me back to the house and pick up your paycheck," she growled.

"That wasn't an option," he reminded her. "Get in, or I will put you in. Those are the choices."

Pure anger replaced the dread she'd known in her room. How dare this insolent hired hand to tell her what she was going to do? He wouldn't dare make her go. That was called kidnapping, and Billy Hawk would have him drawn and quartered for a stunt like that. Or at least hung from the nearest oak tree with a brand-new rope. Mr. Parker might have been given lots of leeway in his job, but today he overstepped his boundaries and picked up his walking papers.

"You wouldn't dare. My daddy will shoot you between the eyes and throw your sorry hide out in the north forty acre for the coyotes' supper if you make me do something I don't want to do," she said bluntly.

"Billy?" Mr. Parker said, his voice traveling back toward the porch.

"Good mornin,' Creole," her father said, as she recognized the sound of a wooden rocking chair's steady rhythm on the porch. "You going shopping this morning? Guess it is about time you left the ranch for a day. Goodness knows I'd never have believed you would stay holed up all these weeks.

Figured you'd already be peeping under those bandages trying to drive yourself by now.''

She couldn't believe her father was in cahoots with this devil she had by the arm. The whole world had just gone mad. ''I'm not going anywhere. Not by myself or with this fool you hired. I'm going back in the house, and I refuse to speak to either of you ever again.'' She stomped her foot hard enough to make dust boil up all the way to her nose.

''Guess I'll pick her up then, Billy,'' Mr. Parker said. ''Not that I'm looking forward to breaking my back on someone sitting around being waited on hand and foot. But suppose a man has to protect his job.''

She saw bright red flashes behind her bandages as fiery fury took over her better judgment. The nerve of these two fellows badgering her to do something she didn't want to do. Well, she'd show both of them. She wasn't afraid of the devil himself, and if it took getting into a stupid pickup truck to prove it, then that is exactly what she would do. She would make Mr. Parker wish he'd been content to take a walk around the ranch this morning. By the end of the day, he'd be yawning with boredom, wanting to crawl into a hole and die from pure, unadulterated doldrums. If he wanted to take her for a ride, then she would exhaust him. Tomorrow he would be content to walk her out to the pond and let her enjoy the morning breeze.

She reached out and touched the open door of the truck, felt for the seat and hopped inside, slamming the door loudly behind her. She didn't see Billy Hawk wink and nod at Parker, who tipped his western hat ever so gently at her father. She just took a deep breath and waited for her heart to stop racing, hoping that it wouldn't jump completely out of her chest when he started the engine and she actually heard the gravel crunch under the wheels.

A heavy silence prevailed in the truck as they drove west toward Allen, where he'd planned a picnic lunch at the park. After the first two minutes, her heart settled down to a steady rhythm, and in her fit of ire, she tried to figure out what he would like to do least on this outing that was so all-fired important.

When the bandages came off her eyes, she planned to hop into her father's truck and drive into Ada, where she would buy a car. Not a truck . . . but why? She questioned her own thoughts. She'd driven a truck since her sixteenth birthday, when Billy gave her a red one. When she traded that one in a couple of years ago, she bought another red one. So why wouldn't she want the same kind now?

Because now I'm terrified of red trucks, she admitted to herself. *They remind me of blood and the red and white semi truck, and all those scary feelings I had at the point of impact. I'm scared it will be bad luck and . . .*

"What color is this truck?" she demanded.

"Dark green," he said.

I'm scared to ride in a red truck again. If he had said it was red, I would have made him take me back to the ranch, even if it made Daddy so mad he wouldn't speak to me for a week. But that's so silly. It wasn't because my truck was red that I had the accident, she argued with herself.

"Where do you want to go?" he asked.

"Back to my room, but evidently that's not an option. You have kidnapped me, and victims don't usually get to call the shots, do they?" She turned her face from him, letting the cool wind from the air-conditioner vent blow across her face. It was like one of those romance books she was addicted to in high school. She was the fair maid whom the dark-haired rogue pirate had snatched off the plantation. Well, the fair maid always won in the end, and she would, too!

"Take me to Ada. I want to go to that little shopping center with the theater. Do you know where that is?" She talked down to him as if he were nothing more than an illiterate field hand.

"Of course, Lady Creole," he snapped back.

''Are we going to see an early matinée?''

She ignored him, glad that she'd finally made him even a little bit angry because she was still having to swallow her wrath, just thinking about the way she'd been submarined into leaving the ranch. Now, just what did all men hate more than anything else in the universe? Shopping. And what could be worse than shopping with a woman who had all her senses intact? The answer was easy— shopping with a blind woman who had to be led by the hand and shown where everything was. She hoped he was savoring his victory, because by the end of the day it wouldn't be nearly so sweet as it was a few minutes ago, when she voluntarily got into his truck and was abducted away.

''First, we will go to the department store there. I want to look at perfumes. My stock is pitifully low. Maybe I'll buy some lotions and bath powder, too. You can hold each one for me while I decide which fragrances I want.'' Her tone was as coldly matter-of-fact.

''Yes, ma'am,'' he said. This was wonderful! He could see how she reacted to different smells. Nothing could be better. He hadn't known how to approach her with the idea of scents, and here it was laid out in his lap just when he figured she was contemplating a way to get even.

Excitement filled her entire body. So he thought

he'd won. Just like Kyle thought he'd won the day he told her he was in love with someone else. Her mind skipped tracks and suddenly wondered what Kyle's new woman looked like. She hoped she was short and had just lost eighty pounds. . . . all of which she would regain two months after the wedding. She smiled, and Parker wondered what on earth she was thinking about but figured it might be best if he didn't know.

''Put it back,'' she demanded when he picked up a sample bottle of perfume on a mirrored tray. ''That is horrid. One spray would overpower a whole room, Mr. Parker.'' She still talked to him like he was a hired hand and she was wearing the crown jewels.

''How about this one?'' He picked up another one, sprayed it into the air above her head and watched her nose twitch as she sniffed. ''Is that better?''

''No, it's ten times worse. Mercy, but I don't remember that fragrance being so strong,'' she admitted. ''Give me a little puff of Youth Dew. That's what I usually wear,'' she said.

''Why do you think it's so strong?'' he asked innocently, wishing he had his little notebook to take a few notes.

''Because I can't see a blessed thing,'' she said.

"If I can't see, then my nose is more sensitive. It doesn't take a psychologist with a Ph.D. to know that, Mr. Parker." She tilted her chin down, a mannerism he remembered from when they were just children, when she told him he was the hired man's son.

"Tell me what you smell," he said.

The clerk behind the counter rolled her eyes in boredom. The woman with the bandages had to have grits for brains for talking to that long, tall, handsome cowboy like he was her servant. The clerk declared silently that she would wear bandages on her eyes if he would lead her around and look at her like Mr. Parker looked at the woman. Then she remembered where she'd seen the lady. She was a regular customer—and she hated to wait on her.

"What happened? You have an accident?" the clerk asked.

"Yes, she did," Mr. Parker said. "A bad auto wreck."

"I can speak for myself," Creole snapped, while the clerk smiled sweetly at Parker, letting him know she understood just how rude this woman could be.

Creole felt the vibes passing from the clerk to her guide and practically turned green with jealousy. She recognized that high-pitched voice with a whiny edge as the one belonging to the gorgeous red-haired clerk she had a personality conflict with every time she walked into this store. And the woman was probably making eyes at her Mr. Parker this very minute.

''I had a car accident and glass got into my eyes. I have to wear these bandages for two more weeks, and then I'll be fine. I think I'll wait until they come off to decide on perfume,'' she said, icicles dripping off her words as she felt for Parker's arm and pulled gently, letting him know she was ready to leave.

''But you haven't inhaled every one of them yet. There is a whole counter of perfume left to test.'' He balked at leaving.

''I know, sweetie,'' she said, honey dripping from her lips. ''But I want to go now. I really need to go to the bathroom, and how are we going to take care of that?''

The clerk shook her head. That crazy woman better wake up and smell the roses, or she was going to lose the handsomest hunk in the whole state of Oklahoma.

''Okay.'' Parker let out a whoosh of air. He hadn't thought about emergency situations like this, but he'd be tarred and feathered before he'd let her get the best of him. ''This way, my lady.''

''How are we going to handle this? I don't know

my way in the ladies' room,'' she said, her voice still sticky sweet with just a touch of mocking laughter.

''Leave it to me. I am at your beck and call. Now, we'll open this door and step right in here. Here is the first stall with a door on it, so your privacy and purity will be protected, Lady Creole.'' He opened the door for her and heaved a sight of relief that no one else was in the restroom.

She felt for the latch to lock the stall door. She hoped a dozen women came into the restroom and found him standing outside the door like a seeing-eye dog. Now why didn't she think of that before? They could have rented a dog for six weeks. It wouldn't have said a smart, sassy word to her, or made her get into a truck against her wishes either.

''All done,'' she said. She unlocked the door and heard a splash somewhere off to her left. Evidently someone had come in, and she was willing to bet that Mr. Parker's face was bright red right at that minute. ''I'm starving to death. Do you intend to feed me today or call the undertaker to cart my carcass to the funeral home?''

''Oh, I've got a nice lunch planned,'' he said, without the smallest trace of embarrassment.

''Good.'' She nodded as they left the store and the warm Oklahoma breeze brushed her hair away from her face. ''And where are we going to eat?''

"You'll see," he answered, opening the door for her and helping her adjust her seat belt.

"No, I won't. What did that lady look like?"

"What lady? That beauty showing us the perfumes?" he asked.

"The one in the bathroom with us," she said.

"Wasn't a lady," he answered with entirely too much amusement.

"What?"

"It was an old man. Do you want to know what his face looked like when he—"

"You took me into the mens' restroom?" she shouted.

"Sure. I wasn't going into the ladies' room. You couldn't see the gentleman, and he didn't care if you borrowed one of the stalls. So we were safe," Parker said.

"You're a cad in the first degree," she said, wishing she could sprinkle a few grains of dust on him and turn him into a toad. But just as sure as she did that, the abominable red-haired clerk would come along and kiss him passionately, turning him back into a—What was Mr. Parker anyway? He sure wasn't a prince, or else he wouldn't have put up with her sass all these weeks. And he wasn't a doctor, or else he wouldn't be working eight hours a day for minimum wages.

*   *   *

Creole was deep in thought when they reached the park on the south side of Allen and Parker stopped the truck. "Are we back at the ranch already? Didn't seem like we'd driven quite long enough," she said, more pleasantly than anything since her "good morning" earlier today.

"Nope, we're at the park. We're going to have a picnic. Julia fixed us up with fried chicken, biscuits and even those apricot fried pies I remember . . ." He rolled his eyes toward the ceiling of the truck and hoped she didn't catch that last word. He really did remember she liked them, but only Johnny Rollin would know that. Good grief! To come this far and then blow his cover over a fried apricot pie.

"You remember? When did I tell you I was addicted to apricot pies?" she said lightly. "Was it the day you said you liked brownies loaded with pecans and with chocolate icing on them? See, I remember what you like, too." She waited for him to open the door.

"Yes, I guess it was that day." He heaved a heavy sigh of relief. Two more weeks and he'd be on his way, but until then, he'd better watch his words a lot more carefully and think before he spoke.

He picked up the basket of food from behind his seat and rounded the back of the pickup, whistling off-key and out of tune as he opened the door for her. ''Take my arm, Creole, and carry this across your other arm.'' He draped a patchwork quilt over her arm and shoulder.

''It's hot,'' she declared. ''I'm going to sweat under these bandages, and the nurse will fuss tonight.''

''It will be worth it,'' Parker said. ''Stand right here and I'll stake our claim to this shady spot under the big oak tree. And then we'll eat.''

''I get both legs.'' She allowed him to lead her and help her get seated.

''Then I get the white meat,'' he retorted.

''Who are you?'' she asked as she bit into the chicken leg. ''Why are you doing this?''

''I'm Mr. Parker. I let you have both legs because I really don't like them, and I'm eating white meat because I'm starving to death after toting you to the store and smelling all that perfume all morning. Any more questions?'' He waited, holding his breath, hoping she couldn't hear the thumping in his chest.

''Oh, hush, if I did have another question, you'd just evade it. Now, what are we going to do all afternoon?''

''Play,'' he said. ''We're in a park with swings and a nice long slide, and if your hearing were a little better, I bet we could even find some rackets and get in a game of tennis. But since you haven't got it fine-tuned enough to hear the ball rush through the air, we'll just have to be content to be little kids again and play on the swings and slide.''

Julia packed enough food for six people, so after lunch he put the leftovers back in the basket, draped a napkin over the top and led Creole to the swings. She giggled when he helped her get situated and squealed when he pushed her, gently at first, then higher and higher until the wind rushed past her face in gusts.

''Mr. Parker.'' She gripped the chains tighter and tighter until he could see her knuckles turning as white as the driven snow. ''Please slow me down. This is worse than a roller-coaster ride,'' she begged.

''Oh, why?'' he pulled back on the swing, slowing her down to a gentle swinging motion.

''Because, you silly fool,'' she chastised. ''I can't see. Remember, that's why you're here. Because I'm blind as a bat, and everything else is intensified. This is really nice, though. Just a nice peaceful swing. I can't remember the last time anyone put me in a swing. . . . must have been back when Johnny and I were little kids and Daddy brought me a swing set for my birthday. Only I really didn't want Johnny to touch it.''

''No one swung you in grade school?'' he asked,

steering the conversation away from himself.

"Oh, sure. Andrea and I rushed out to play on the swings every day at recess," she said.

"Andrea?"

"My best friend in the whole world. We started kindergarten together and stayed close all through school. Then we went to East Central over at Ada together and graduated from there last year," she said.

"Why hasn't she come to see you while you've been out of commission?" he asked. "If she's your best friend, where's she been?"

"On her honeymoon," Creole told him in an exasperated tone. "She and Tom got married two days before I had this accident. We'd just finished the summer session and got our master's degrees. I was her maid of honor. And then they left for a tour of Europe for a whole month for their honeymoon. She probably doesn't even know about the accident. But she'll be home this weekend, and they'll be in church. Hey, why don't you take me to church on Sunday? Daddy could take me, but he's got a cattle auction in Dallas this weekend. Then you can meet her." The swing slowed until it was barely moving. "Parker!" she raised her voice, a sudden surge of fear surrounding her. "Where are you?"

"Right here," he said just inches from her face.

"I was listening. I'd be glad to take you to church on Sunday. Baptist?"

"Yes, the big one on Main Street," she told him. "Momma is Catholic and I go to Mass when I'm down there, but when I'm home, Daddy and I are Baptist." She sighed, letting the tension out of her muscles. "I think I'm ready for a nap now. Did you bring a pillow?"

"Yes, I did." He took her arm. "I'll stay awake and protect us from rattlesnakes and bears and coyotes."

"And big black spiders?" she said seriously.

"You are afraid of spiders? I thought you were big and mean and tough and would fight a forest fire with a cup of water." He laughed.

"I am all of the above. And spiders are more ferocious than a forest fire so they're to be feared more. Just keep a close watch for them while I sleep, and when I wake up, we can go home, can't we?"

"Yes, Lady Creole," he intoned in mock seriousness. "We can go back to the ranch, since you have so graciously admitted that you will leave again come Sunday morning."

"And if I hadn't?" She laid her head back on the pillow and stretched out, folding her hands across her tummy, making him wish he could meet her again when she was sighted so she could know who he really was. But that could never, ever happen. Especially now that he'd pulled this trick on her.

"Then you would have had to brave the elements with only me for protection until you came to your senses and realized nothing was going to happen to you outside the four walls of your bedroom, or your safe haven of a ranch," he said. She heard a bit of longing or pain in his voice, and wondered what she'd said to cause it.

Chapter Five

Julia helped Creole find a brightly colored broom stick skirt in swirling colors of red, purple, yellow and blue. The matching soft-knit tunic in bright red added color to her cheeks and made her jet black hair shine with luster. She was strapping a pair of purple kid leather sandals on her feet when she heard Parker's footsteps in the hallway. A grin played at the corners of her mouth. She wished she could see him this morning. From the way that sales clerk flirted with him she knew, he wasn't bald, ancient or disgusting, and curiosity had kept her awake long after she went to bed last night.

"My, oh my," Parker exclaimed appreciatively, without a hint of sarcasm in his voice. "Don't you look lovely. All you need are silver bracelets on your arms and a scarf around your head, and I do believe you could play the beautiful Gypsy in a movie.''

''Cajun,'' she reminded him, rewarding him with a sincere, bright smile that showed off beautiful, even teeth. ''Not Gypsy, but Cajun.''

He took her arm just like always, looping it through his, patting her fingertips across his biceps. ''I better get a big stick to beat off the young men who are going to try to rob me of my job today. One look at you and they'll be lined up for miles, begging for an interview.''

''I'm so sure,'' she said. ''They'd probably want to read to me, and I'd gag. I can't wait to get to church and see Andrea. She called me when we got back from the park, and she couldn't believe the story of the wreck. She's coming over for supper tomorrow night. Tom has a meeting at the college, so she's free for the evening. You can have a little time off. I'm sure you wouldn't want to listen to girl talk for hours on end, and we're planning to catch up. Is this your truck?'' She felt for the door.

''Sure is.'' He opened the door and helped her inside. ''So Andrea has been your best friend since kindergarten? You didn't know her before you went to school?'' He asked cautiously, hoping the girl didn't remember Johnny Rollin from the days when Hank and Martha took him to the Baptist

Church, and praying that none of the old timers in the church would remember him. Hank was off to the cattle sale with Billy this morning, so no one would look at his father and at him, and put two and two together. He and his father were the same height, shared the same black hair and slight cleft in their chins, but Parker had his mother's soft gray eyes and a rounder face than Hank.

"Nope. She and her family moved to Allen the summer before we started school. She was crying and holding onto her mother's skirt, and I walked up to her and told her to quit being such a baby. I told her that her mother would be waiting for her after school and took her by the hand. We ran off to the playground and were best friends from then on," she told him as they drove down the lane. She was amazed that she didn't have a trace of an anxiety attack—no fluttering butterflies in her stomach, not a single missed heartbeat, and she didn't even hold her breath for one second. She'd surely come a long way since the first day Mr. Parker stepped into her bedroom and declared she was blind, not helpless.

"Penny for your thoughts," he said, glad that his job would be secure for a couple more weeks. His thesis was almost finished now, and he was pleased with his efforts. There was a job opportunity opening up in Ada, but he really didn't know if he wanted to be that close to the Cajun Gypsy beside him when the storm hit. She was going to erupt like a volcano if she ever found out that she'd kept company with her arch enemy for all those weeks.

"My thoughts would cost you far more than a penny. You'd have to sell this truck, put a mortgage on your personal belongings, and sign over your checks for the past month just to get close to my thoughts," she said.

"Must be pretty serious," he said.

"Yep, they are," she nodded. "Are we almost there? Andrea said she'd wait outside the church for me. I'm so excited! Mercy, this is the longest we've been separated since we were five. That's eighteen years."

Andrea's hair was the same color as Creole's, but that's where the resemblance ended. Andrea was five-feet-two inches tall, slightly overweight and had a faint sprinkling of freckles across her nose. She and Creole acted like they were still in elementary school, patting each other and hugging, both talking at once and ignoring everyone else, including Tom and Parker.

"Tom Whittensell." The tall, lanky man with thin blond hair stuck out his hand.

"Parker." He shook, with the man, hoping he didn't press for a last name. The longer he kept company with Creole, the harder it was to keep himself in the clear.

"Glad to meet you. Guess we won't get a word in edgewise. Bet they whisper all during services and don't listen to a word." He grinned.

"Well, Creole's been pretty excited about seeing her friend again. She's been feeling isolated lately," Parker said.

"Time to go in." Tom took Andrea by the arm. "We'll be late."

Parker picked up Creole's arm and led her up the walk into the sanctuary. "Where do you want to sit?"

"With Andrea, of course. Put us between you and Tom so we can whisper if we remember something important," she told him.

"Yes, ma'am." He couldn't keep the grin off his face.

Creole sang the first hymn from memory, not missing a note or a word, her soft voice like pure honey in Parker's ear. He remembered the tune she sang when they danced in the field after Kyle broke up with her. He shut his eyes, visualizing her in a pair of faded jeans and T-shirt as they two-stepped in the scorched brown grass. And he daydreamed desperately for a time when he could really dance with her—not as Mr. Parker, her caretaker, but as Johnny Rollin. A time when she would lay her head on his chest and listen to the fast beating of his heart, even though he was the hired man's son. But there would be a blizzard in August on Hawk Ridge before that happened, so he'd just as well open his eyes and face reality. There wouldn't ever be a day when Amanda Creole Hawk and John Parker Rollin would dance together in the field, while she sang an old Cajun love ballad to him.

"Where in the world did Billy find Mr. Parker?" Andrea whispered softly when the preacher started his sermon on the commandment about lying and the effects of not telling the truth.

"Why?"

"Hasn't anyone told you about him?" Andrea couldn't believe her friend didn't even know what the man looked like. Surely Julia had been singing his praises and Billy Hawk had told her that he was about their age.

"No, what about him?"

"Mercy me," Andrea said. "He's just movie star good-looking is all. He's got hair as black as yours, and a cleft in his chin. Hollywood would probably fight over which studio got him if he ever crossed the California line. And honey, the way he looks at you just makes me swoon."

"Oh, hush, he's hired help and he doesn't look at me except as a patient." But Creole felt the heat of a blush rising from her neck.

"I wouldn't care if he was an illiterate cotton picker. You better brand him before he gets away," Andrea whispered.

"Not on your life. He's egotistical—"

"Another plus. You'd never be happy with a wimp. Look at what happened with Kyle. I told you in the beginning he was just a wimp. You should have listened to me, and if you know what's good for you, you'll pay attention now. Mr. Parker is your soulmate. I know it just by looking at him. Since you can't see, I'll be your eyes. For crying out loud, Creole, don't let him get away from you. You two look like you were made for each other."

"You've just come from your honeymoon so you have got love in your eyes. I think I'll just wait until these bandages come off and see for myself. I don't know a single thing about him," she whispered back.

"With eyes like those, who cares?" Andrea said. "And when you can see, you'll find out I was right. He fills out those starched jeans so good, old Mary Beth's having trouble listening to the preacher. She keeps sneaking peeks across the aisle and I'd be willing to bet you that she's devising a way to get an invitation to the ranch next week. She's probably kicking herself right now for not coming out to visit you every day. And Lucy has this big old grin on her face like the cat who ate the canary. You better keep him at home these next two weeks, or else you're going to have to fight your way through a maze of women just to get a chance at him. And that's all I've got to say.''

Creole tried to listen to the rest of the sermon, but her thoughts kept sneaking down the Mr. Parker path and what Andrea said about him. Probably when the bandages came off her eyes and she could see him with more than her fingertips, she would find him just as plain as Tom Whittensell. That Andrea had just been bitten by the love bug and was looking at the situation through rose-colored glasses.

It would be interesting to see just what he did look like physically. Goodness knows he was obstinate enough to be overconfident and handsome. He hadn't let her win a single battle in the weeks he'd been there to keep her company, not even when she threatened to fire him if he made her ride in his truck. And she was dependent upon him. . . . But dependency didn't constitute love, and many a marriage had landed on the sharp rocks in the sea of life when the two got mixed up. *Good grief,* she chastised herself, *here I am thinking about a future with a man I don't even know. He could be married or divorced six times or engaged to some beauty from wherever he'll go back to when this job is finished. But by then, at least I'll have a face to go with that exciting voice that says, "Good morning, Creole," every day.*

Parker's ears picked up something about branding and a maze of women, but that's all the girl talk he got, which wasn't much. They were probably whispering about the honeymoon and something that happened in Europe during the past month. He recognized a couple of men about his father's age who looked at him quizzically. But no one approached him after church, and he was thankful for that. Later, maybe at Thanksgiving, he would attend church with his father and they'd remember him. By then, Creole would be in a snit and off in Louisiana with her mother. At least he wouldn't have to put up with her snubs during his visit. *But when you walk through the pasture and remember the dance and her voice, and when you sit in this very sanctuary and remember the way your heart feels right now sitting beside her, it's not going to be easy*, he reminded himself.

"See you tomorrow." Andrea hugged Creole quickly one last time after she was in the truck. "We have to go to lunch with the Whittensell family. They want to hear all about the honeymoon, they say. I could make them drop with heart attacks, but I'll be good and tell them about the scenery and show them the pictures. You should see my photo of Big Ben. I got the camera crooked and it looks more like the leaning tower of Pisa.'' She talked non-stop. ''I'll show them all to you in a couple of weeks, and we'll catch up more tomorrow.'' She slammed the door and was off like a sprite with her husband, her arm looped in his, much like Creole's rested in Parker's when they went for walks.

''Take me home. I'm starving.'' Creole giggled lightheartedly.

''Nope, we're going out to lunch. Billy said if I took you to a café, then Julia could have the day off,'' Parker said.

''I can't.'' Creole's tone changed to one of fear again.

''And why can't you?'' Parker asked.

''I'll embarrass you and myself. When it's just us, you can help me see where the food is. We'd be in a place with people.'' She fumbled for the words to make him understand.

''Not where we're going. Honey, I don't have an unlimited bank account, and this is on me, not your father. We're going to the best place in the world for a good old chili burger and french fries. And maybe even a ice cream sundae afterwards. I might embarrass you before the meal is finished. I'm wearing a freshly starched white shirt. Can't you just see chili stains all over the front of it?'' he said.

''And where is this wonderful place?'' she asked, her fear suddenly replaced by curiosity and hunger.

''The café on the end of the Citgo station out on the highway,'' he told her. ''You know, where you probably went for burgers during your lunch breaks in high school.''

She smiled. Only Mr. Parker would take her to a place like that for lunch after church. Any other man would have reservations at a steak house. ''Okay, but you'll have to help me,'' she said.

''That's my job,'' he said, and she heard that same loneliness she'd heard at the park a couple of days before.

The onions she smelled frying on the grill when he opened the door made her mouth water. It had been months since she'd been in this place, and the last time it was to quickly grab a bag of chips and a bottle of water. She couldn't remember the last time she ate a greasy onion burger with a side of french fries.

''Mmmmm,'' she moaned. ''I don't want chili on my burger. Tell them to put it in a bowl. I want a good old-fashioned burger. You better have lots of money in your bank account because I'm going to put you in the poor house, I'm so hungry," she said as he pulled out a chair and seated her at one of the small tables.

"Hey, Creole Hawk, I heard about your accident. Sorry about that," the young waitress said.

"I'm sorry, I don't recognize your voice." Creole smiled.

"I'm Becky. My Dad is foreman over at the Fleming ranch next to Hawk Ridge." She set plastic glasses of water in front of Parker and Creole. "What can I get you two today?"

"Burgers," Creole said, reaching cautiously for the water and sipping it. "With lots of onions and a bowl of chili on the side. French fries and the biggest glass of tea you got. Parker?"

"Same," he said. "I'm going to the men's room, Creole. I'll be right back." He reassured her with a pat on the arm.

"Whew, where did you find him? And is there any more where he came from?" Becky said softly when he was out of hearing distance.

"Daddy hired him to take care of me while I'm out of commission. Drive me, talk to me, whatever. Why do you ask?"

"Oh, Creole, you should see him. He looks like a model out of one of those magazines for men's clothing. He's just the most handsome man I've ever seen, and those eyes . . . I'd lay down in the middle of the highway and die happy if he'd look at me like he just did you.'' Becky giggled breathlessly.

''What about his eyes?'' Creole asked.

''They're a funny color, but they're so beautiful they make my heart race,'' Becky told her. ''Here he comes, so I'll get busy on your order. If you don't want him when you get your bandages off, just pass him on to me. He might be a couple of years older than me, but. . . .''

''Wait a minute. What funny color are his eyes?'' Creole whispered. He wasn't close enough for her to smell his woodsy shaving lotion, or to hear the heels of his boots on the tile floor, so maybe Becky could tell her more.

''Not blue, not green, almost gray,'' Becky said softly. ''No color at all. And he looks at you so sweet. Oh, there you are. I didn't catch your name,'' Becky said loudly.

''It's Parker, Mr. Parker,'' he said, aware that they'd been talking about him, hoping that Becky had never seen him before and wasn't busy blowing his cover.

''Well, I'm glad to meet you, Mr. Parker. Don't be a stranger around here. We make the best hamburgers in the whole county,'' Becky said flirtatiously.

''Yes, ma'am.'' He smiled. ''You're going to

have to slaughter another steer if you don't hurry up and get the order cooked. Creole is hungry.''
He ignored the waitress and stared at Creole with such a soft expression that Becky swore silently if a man ever looked at her like that she intended to hogtie him and drag him to the nearest justice of the peace.

Chapter Six

Parker laced his hands behind his head, kicked the top sheet off his long legs and stared at the ceiling, which became a king-sized screen for a mental video of the past five weeks. There was Creole that first day, sitting in the darkness of her bedroom, afraid to even try dressing herself. Slowly she progressed through the weeks, until she stood before him today, the old Creole, sassy, full of spit and vinegar in spite of her sightlessness. She'd learned to depend on her other senses to get around the house and to draw confidence from when confronted with new situations, like eating in a restaurant.

The picture on the ceiling changed, and she was sitting beside the pond with her knees drawn up, her arms wrapped around them, telling him that she had been refolding her pajamas just so she could touch the fabric. That her fingertips were becoming eyes and that she could tell the grass was brown because green grass felt different. She wore faded jeans and a red T-shirt and the never-ending Oklahoma breeze fanned her black hair away from her delicate face.

Then there she was fingering the drapes on the day Kyle made her so mad she could chew up two by fours and spit out toothpicks. That was when she told him that she had a whole barrel of anger she'd like to unleash on someone. Well, after she found out she'd been telling her heart's secrets to Johnny Rollin, she might have a keg of dynamite she'd rope him to and then light the fuse. He smiled, thinking about the man who would finally come along and win her heart. He'd have a lifetime of hard work cut out for him, but he'd never endure a day of boredom. She'd keep him on his toes and make him work for every bit of affection she ever gave him. The smile faded when he thought about Creole wrapping her arms around another man.

He fluffed his pillow, sighed and fell backwards with a thud. A blink or two and her vision appeared again. This time in that Gypsy skirt and long, soft blouse when they went to church two weeks ago. A cute little grin played at the corners of her full mouth when she and Andrea exchanged private whispers. Meanwhile he had really tried to pay attention to the sermon, which was about lying and deception. What a choice of subjects as he sat there beside her. She had no idea he was Johnny Rollin, the boy she'd hated since childhood.

The khaki walking shorts she wore yesterday showed off her long legs. She'd come so far from that first morning when she got her shirt on backwards.

His thesis was finished, and he was happy with his work. The hard copy was printed, bound in the proper form, a computer disk inserted into the side pocket of the binder ready to be delivered tomorrow afternoon. His appointment was at three-thirty in Texas with his advisor, who sounded eager to see him and glad that he had indeed finished the paper and didn't need an extension. But he wondered if he'd paid too dear a price for the thesis. Because now his heart didn't want to leave, although his mind knew he must. Tomorrow while he was waiting in the outer office for his appointment, Creole would be waiting in the doctor's office for the bandages to come off her eyes.

And neither Mr. Parker nor Johnny Rollin would be there.

*   *   *

Creole laced her hands behind her head, too excited to sleep. In less than twenty-four hours, the bandages were coming off for the last time—and this time, she'd get to open her eyes. Billy Hawk and Parker would be standing close by, and she'd finally get to see the man who'd become her friend in these past weeks. Andrea kept telling her she'd better take a pair of sunglasses because she was going to be plumb dazzled by Parker. But even if he was ugly, he'd kept her on her toes during this difficult time. He'd pulled her out of a deep pity pool, made her mad enough to face the ranch and then the world beyond it, and finally woke her up to the fact she could really rejoice in the fact that she was alive and the blindness was just a temporary discomfort.

She didn't have a face to go with the deep voice she'd come to know these past weeks. But she remembered the first time she heard that voice, when she told him he could leave, that she wouldn't have a man waiting on her. Tonight she was glad he'd been obstinate and said she wasn't helpless just because she couldn't see.

He'd told her that first day that she could trust him. And he'd proven in a million little ways as well as a few great big ways that she could trust without fear. He'd been there when Kyle proved to be a jerk. She put her hand over her heart, feeling the steady beat and remembering the way his heart raced when she insisted he dance with her out in the pasture. Did she really have that kind of effect on him? Or was it fear of not being able to dance, even though he did it so well?

She could hear his boots stepping down the hall in her imagination. And him telling her they were going out for the day. She could feel the wind blowing in her face as he swung her higher and higher, and she felt her trust for him to keep the monster spiders at bay while she took a long after-noon nap.

I can't see him, but my heart can. And the heart doesn't have eyes, she told herself. *It depends on all the other senses to see for it. So what do my other senses tell me? That's he's been dependable, steady and trustworthy. And who knows what will happen tomorrow, when these cursed bandages are removed and I can really see him. I'll just have to keep an open mind—and shoot Andrea if she's been pulling my leg this whole time!*

''Good morning, Creole.'' His voice sounded a bit tired when he opened the door.

''Mr. Parker.'' She'd already been out to the kitchen for breakfast, had a shower and was dressed for the morning. She had a CD in the player and was listening to Shania Twain, realizing that what she and Kyle had was just a passing fancy that could scarcely even be called love.

"You're getting pretty self-sufficient these days." His voice was actually a little hoarse. He sounded like he was having trouble with his words.

"Yep, I am. You better be glad this job is over because I might not have needed you anymore, even if I wasn't getting all this off today," she teased.

"It's been a good job, Creole. I'm glad to have had it. I just want you to know that," he said.

"Mercy, you sound serious. I can't believe you'd be serious, Mr. Parker. Not the man who threatened to pick me up and put me in the truck." She laughed, but it didn't ring true. Something was wrong this morning. Mr. Parker was about to tell her something and she wasn't sure she wanted to hear it.

"I am very serious. I just wanted to say a couple of things this morning before I leave. I have enjoyed this job, and even though we've fought often, we've laughed just as often and—"

"Leave?" she shouted.

"Yes, I'm leaving in about ten minutes. I've got an appointment in . . . well, with an important person this afternoon, so I'm leaving," he said.

"But you're going with me to the doctor. You're going to be there for the grand finale when they take these off.'' She touched the white gauze covering her eyes. ''We're going out with Daddy to celebrate afterwards. Steaks and the whole nine yards. I've planned it all week.''

''Sorry, honey. I'll have to miss the whole nine yards.'' He tried to chuckle but it didn't come out very convincingly. What on earth was wrong with him anyway? This was Amanda Creole Hawk, the meanest little girl in the universe and the sassiest, hardest-to-live-with woman ever born into the race. Why was saying goodbye so difficult?

''You told me I could trust you,'' she whispered, vengeance pouring out of her tone like lava from the top of a volcano.

''You could and you did. I never once told you I'd be here on the day you were sighted again, did I?'' His own voice rose with rage, replacing the lump in his throat.

''No, but you said I could trust you and I did. Now when it's time for me to see you for who you really are, you run away. Who is this important person? Are you married, Mr. Parker?''

''Nope,'' he answered.

''Engaged? Have you got a fiancée on the back burner who would have a fit if she knew you'd been babysitting some rancher's daughter?''

''Nope,'' he said.

''Then who is so blasted important that they

couldn't wait just one more day? You owe me that much, Mr. Parker. Today is my big day, and I want you there,'' she hissed, anger boiling up to cover the hurt in her heart.

''You're used to getting what you want, Creole, but trust me, you don't really want me there,'' he said, and she heard that loneliness in his voice she'd heard twice before. ''This is your glory day, and you'll do fine. Go out and buy yourself a brand-new red pickup truck. Don't be afraid of it bringing you bad luck. I know that's what you thought when you asked me what color my truck was. I lied—it's cranberry red. Just a shade darker than the one you kissed the semi truck with, and not one thing happened all the times you rode in it.''

''You lied to me!'' The volume was back. ''You sorry rascal. How many other lies have you told me? I bet you even eat Brussels sprouts.'' She threw the words at him like bullets from the end of a high-powered rifle.

''Nope, I hate the little green devils.'' He laughed, making her even angrier.

''You're afraid for me to see you,'' she argued. ''What's wrong with you? Do you have a wart on the end of your nose with big hairs growing out of it?''

''Wrong again, but right on one issue. I'm not

going to be there, and that's a fact, Lady Creole. You've got a life to get back to. It's been an experience these past few weeks. Take care of yourself, Creole Hawk,'' he said, and she could hear his voice getting closer and closer to her chair.

''Then go, and don't look back.'' She set her mouth in a desperate effort to control the quiver in her chin. She approached hard situations with anger, not tears, and she'd be hung from the nearest oak tree before she let him see a single tear drip down her cheeks. It wasn't fair—to drop into her life from nowhere, then to disappear back into the vapor of nothingness again. She was ferociously protective of her friends and she'd put him in that category these past weeks.

''Goodbye, Amanda Creole Hawk,'' he whispered close enough that she could feel his breath on her ear, making her shiver. Then he leaned down and kissed her ever so gently on her forehead, heat flowing from his firm mouth like a branding iron, leaving an imprint just below her hairline as indelibly as the one already burned into her heart.

She bit her lip and turned away from him so he wouldn't see the stinging tears flowing down her cheeks.

''Hello, Creole,'' Andrea's voice came over the phone line. ''Are you ready to see again today?''

"I guess so," Creole said.

"What do you mean, you guess so?" Andrea asked.

"Mr. Parker left this morning. He's not going to be there, Andrea. And I wanted to see him, really see him. So I guess I'm ready to see again, but I won't see what I wanted to see, so it's a hard question. One I never thought I'd have to think about. This day has lasted forever. Julia popped in with lunch, and Daddy will be here in an hour to take me to the doctor, but all I've had is memories and Shania Twain to keep me sane. He's gone, Andrea, and I miss him," she said honestly.

"Oh, he'll come back. He looked at you with pure love flowing out of his whole body. I'm not wrong, Creole. He'll show up at the doctor's office. Maybe he's going to surprise you. Look for the gorgeous man in starched jeans and either a western shirt or a T-shirt with a pocket. Just open your pretty green eyes and look around the room for the man with the strangely beautiful eyes. That will be him." Andrea giggled, sure that Mr. Parker would indeed be there on this important day.

"I hope you're right, but I heard something in his voice that makes me believe he's really gone for good," Creole said. "I'll call you tonight and tell you what it's like to see the world again."

"We'll be out at a dinner until late, but I'll wait

up for your call," Andrea said. "Good luck. If you look across that room and the sparks are there, you'll know it's him," she teased.

"Sure," Creole said as she placed the phone down. It wasn't going to be that way. From the very bottom of her heart she knew he was gone, and she knew she would never see Mr. Parker again. When she was an old woman with gray streaks in her hair, bent over a cane, she would tell her granddaughter about the time she was blind and an angel dropped out of the sky to take care of her. She might even compose a Cajun ballad about him. But she'd never see him again and that was a fact.

Creole bowed her head and let the tears flow freely. She heard her heart shatter into a million ragged pieces in the wake of the smell of a woodsy aftershave lotion still floating through the air, a husky voice telling her goodbye, and the burn on her forehead where his lips kissed her for the first, the only and the final time.

Chapter Seven

The doctor did just what the nurse did every day. Except that instead of telling her to keep her eyelids tightly closed until he could get on a new bandage, he put some drops into her eyes and encouraged her to make the muscles work and open her eyes up wide. The room was dark, but still she blinked several times trying to focus on anything in the darkness. There were forms she supposed were people but they were somewhere beyond a misty gray fog.

"Well?" the doctor said.

"I don't know what to expect," she said honestly.

"Neither do I," he said. "Every patient reacts differently. I'm going to shine a penlight into your eyes now to make sure they've healed properly,'' he said as he flashed a small light into her eyes as he held it open. It looked like the oncoming head- light of a car during a rainstorm, prisms going every which way, but it didn't really hurt. "Looks good. Real good as a matter of fact. You did just what I told you, except the bandages were a little wet. Guess you got them in the shower a bit today?''

"No sir.'' She swallowed the lump in her throat. Was one of those people standing over there against the wall Mr. Parker? If it was, she might give him a scathing piece of her mind as soon as he identified himself. Tears welled up in her eyes and spilled over her heavy black lashes down her cheeks. She wanted to hit something or someone. If the anger inside her didn't settle down pretty quick, they'd have to clean her off a spot right here in the examining room so she could throw a first- rate hissy fit.

"Hurting?'' he asked, turning off the penlight.

"No sir,'' she said. "Just glad to be able to see even a little bit, I guess,'' she said weakly.

"Will you please turn the dimmer up very, very slowly,'' he said to the lady in the background, who was beginning to look more like a person than a white blob.

When the first light made dark shadows on the

walls, she recognized her father. He was smiling brightly. She'd never seen his weathered face look so handsome, and all the anger left in a whoosh. If she never saw Mr. Parker again, at least she was alive and she still had a father who'd stood beside her all through the years. He'd always been there— even when her mother just wanted her for a few visits a year. It was Billy Hawk who rocked her when she had pneumonia as a child and couldn't sleep. He was the one who stayed up late when she went out on her first date to be sure she got home by curfew. He was there when she graduated from high school and college and who beamed when she got her master's degree last summer. It was his voice she heard in the darkness when she awoke from the wreck. And there he was right now with that silly grin she loved so much on his face.

Tears filled her eyes again and spilled over her cheeks as she searched the dim room for a tall, handsome man with strangely beautiful eyes. But he didn't materialize. The doctor and nurse were the only other people in the room with her. She resolved in those next minutes that she wouldn't think about it anymore. Like Scarlett O'Hara in the book she loved, she'd think about it tomorrow.

But somehow her heart didn't get the message, and it grieved for what could not be. One part was furious at him for skipping out on her; the other part was crushed. And all of Creole just wanted to go home to the ranch, curl up in her recliner and get the whole mess sorted out so she could live with it.

"You must wear sunglasses when you're out in the daytime for several months," the doctor was saying. "Your eyes will be sensitive, but I'm glad to see the tear ducts working so well. Sometimes they are damaged and the patient has to use artificial tears, but I believe you'll be fine. Unless you have any problems, I think you can wait until after Thanksgiving for a check-up, Miss Hawk. Then it'll just be a routine check so we can dismiss you. You're a very lucky girl. Things could have been much worse. Take care of those pretty brown eyes, now." He patted her on the shoulder. "Get her a pair of those sleek dark lensed sunglasses. You'll be amazed how much light they block," he said as he left.

"So should we go home, or are you hungry?" Billy asked when they got outside.

Hungry? Her stomach would rebel and pitch anything she tried to swallow right back out. She took a deep breath and tried to make the disappointment disappear. She was acting like a child who didn't get the little red wagon she wanted on Christmas morning. This was absolutely ridiculous. She was twenty-three years old. She'd had lots of dates in the years since she was sixteen, when her father finally consented to let her go out for the first time. Sure, she'd always gotten almost everything she'd ever wanted, and today was a disappointment. But she'd gotten over losing a mother, and she'd learned to deal with the fact that her mother didn't want her on a full-time basis, disrupting her perfect little political life in New Orleans. She'd lived with six weeks of blindness and an obstinate idiot who wouldn't even stay a few hours longer so she could thank him properly for helping her through a tough time. So she'd survive today—and she'd do it with her chin up and her old brassy attitude. And Mr. Parker could take a long walk off a short pier!

"Well?" Her father started the engine and looked across the seat at her. Something had changed. The insolence was gone from her eyes. Strange, he'd never thought when they took the bandages off he'd see a new daughter. He expected the same girl who argued a blue streak when she didn't get her way, the one who fired five women in five days and barely tolerated Johnny Rollin these past five weeks. But when she took the sunglasses off to flick a piece of lint from the lens there was a softness in her eyes, reminding Billy of her Cajun grandmother, Evangelina's mother. She'd died right after Billy and Evangelina married, but he remembered the tall, stately woman well, and when Creole was born he didn't have any reservations naming her after Evangelina's mother.

"Let's go home, Daddy," she said. "I want to look at Hawk Ridge. I want to see the horses, and take a long walk by myself through the pastures."

She pulled her hair up in a ponytail and changed into a pair of cut-off jean shorts and pink T-shirt. She jerked on a pair of comfortable, well-worn sneakers, set her sunglasses on her nose and waved at her father who was enjoying a tall glass of iced tea on the front porch. She needed this time to come to grips with this new person. It was as if Creole Hawk had changed in the space of a few weeks, but more literally in the blink of an eye in a doctor's waiting room. She was going to walk until dark on this late summer night, and when she got home there was going to be peace in her heart. . . . or at least resolution if she couldn't find peace.

The frogs and crickets were battling for front stage as they sang their summer songs. Before long, winter would arrive and they'll go wherever frogs and crickets hole up for the bitter cold months, but tonight they sang to Creole. She didn't understand their language anymore than she understood this restless feeling deep inside her heart, but she could appreciate their efforts.

She realized Glory, the ranch's blue heeler cow

dog, was following her, but she didn't fuss at him. The dog had a blue eye and a brown one. She remembered both Becky and Andrea saying something about Mr. Parker having strange eyes. Maybe he had a blue one and a brown one. She laughed at that thought and wondered just exactly what they did mean. Andrea said something about spit-colored eyes—whatever that was. Perhaps they were like Martha Rollin's eyes. Kind of pale gray and witchy looking. Probably they were that strange light shade of blue that she'd seen a few times. They were kind of haunting, but they didn't look like Mrs. Rollin's. Mercy, when she looked at Creole, it was like she could see right into her very soul.

She walked the fence line, counting cows and calves, whistling at the horses to watch their ears perk up. When dark came, she had tired feet and an urge to crawl into a bathtub full of sudsy bubbles, but there wasn't peace in her heart. However, she'd made one resolution, and that was that she was going to settle down on this ranch and start helping her father run it. After all, it would be hers someday. It was high time she grew up—time to be an adult and learn the ropes because someday Billy Hawk wouldn't be there, and she'd need to fill his boots.

* * *

''Well, did he show up?'' Andrea asked late that night when Creole phoned her.

''No. I didn't think he would. There was a definite finish to his voice when he said good-bye this morning,'' she said flatly. ''But I can see, and the leaves are green, and Glory kept me company when I took a walk. And I'm going to start to work tomorrow for the ranch.''

''You are what? I thought you were going to New Orleans to find a job. Is this the girl who was going into politics or high business?'' Andrea couldn't believe her ears.

''Yes, it is. Tomorrow I'm doing what I should have done a while back. I got an education in business with a minor in agriculture just in case I ever needed it. Well, Andrea, I need it. Hawk Ridge is going to be mine someday. So I'm going to learn how to run it. And while we're at it, just what was it about Mr. Parker's eyes that you kept talking about?''

''I don't know. They were this funny shade of something. Kind of like the sky on a rainy day, I guess, or more like the sky just before a hard snow. I just never saw anything like them. But it wasn't just the color, Creole. It was the way he looked at you. I just knew you two were soulmates. One of those matches made up in heaven that lasts forever,'' she said.

"Well, I guess you were wrong this time. Come see me next week when you have time. Or call me and we'll meet somewhere for lunch. I don't know how busy Daddy will keep me. Probably make me work like a field hand to try to scare me away. He wants a southern belle for a daughter, but I guess he'll have to be satisfied with a hired hand."

Parker handed his thesis to his advisor and sat back in the soft burgundy leather chair on the other side of the desk. "Here it is, sir. Hope it passes muster," he said.

"I'm sure it will, Parker. Tell me, though, how in the world did you find a real live subject to work with you?"

"It was a fluke, sir," Parker said. "Just a fluke. My dad is foreman of Hawk Ridge, a pretty big spread in Oklahoma. I went there for a month to work on my paper in solitude, and the owner's daughter had just been involved in an accident. I asked for the job of caring for her." He cleared his throat. "Just a fluke," he repeated.

"A mighty lucky one. I'll be looking forward to reading this." He stood up and shook Parker's hand. "Still working at the same place.?"

"Yes, but there is a job opening up close to my dad I'm considering," he said, surprising himself. He'd argued with that niggling little voice inside his head all the way back to Denton, and he thought he'd finally won the battle. He would never set foot in Oklahoma again until he was sure Creole was safely in Louisiana with her mother. And only then would he visit Hawk Ridge.

He threw open the door to his apartment, dragged in his garment bags and suitcases and tossed them on the sofa. Creole's bandages would be off by now, and she'd be back at the ranch, probably issuing orders and demanding that Billy Hawk take her into town tomorrow for a brand-new vehicle. The thought of her in a red truck flitted through his mind and made his heart ache.

"Well, I know how to fix that," he said aloud, reaching for the telephone and dialing a familiar number.

"Hello," a feminine voice said on the other end.

"Vicky?" he said.

"Parker, you old devil," she giggled. "Did you finish that paper you had to go hide out in the hinterlands to do? Are you finally back in the land of the living?"

"I sure am." He tried to smile but it didn't reach his eyes.

"Well, ask me out to dinner then," she demanded. "Like tonight. I can be ready in five minutes."

"I can't, but if you'll give me an hour I'll pick you up. Steak or lobster?"

"I'll decide while I'm doing my nails," she said.

A bundle of red-haired energy met him at the door of her two-story house. She wrapped both arms around his neck and pulled his mouth down to hers for a passionate kiss. "Mmmmm," she mumbled, and he remembered the day Creole made the same noise when she smelled onions frying on the grill in the little café inside the Citgo station.

"Miss me?" he asked, shaking the memory from his mind.

"Oh, honey, you don't know how much," she mumbled huskily in his ear. "But right now I'm starving. You kept me waiting five minutes more than an hour and I have to have food or I'm going to starve. You won't have anything to tell me since you've been tied to a computer and a stack of research books for more than a month, so I'll catch you up on the crowd and all the gossip." She grabbed her purse, locked the door and slipped her hand in his. "I'll drive. You know I hate jumping up in that blasted truck you insist on driving. I've ruined two kick pleats in my straight skirts doing that, and I'll not do it again. Let's eat lobster. Bet you've lived on bologna sandwiches and pork and beans all summer, too." She opened the door to her Porsche and he folded his tall body into the passenger's seat.

She rambled on about mutual friends while they ate their way through an appetizer plate and drank two glasses of iced tea each. She criticized the waitress and complained that the restaurant didn't serve white wine, but Parker only listened with one ear. He was sitting across the linen-covered table with the richest, most eligible lady in all of north central Texas. The one who could take her pick of dozens and dozens of rich bachelors. But everything she said, everything she did, even the perfume she wore, made him remember something else about Creole Hawk.

He'd called Vicky, thinking she'd erase all thoughts of Creole. She'd entertain him, tell him the area news and then he wouldn't even think about Hawk Ridge again until Thanksgiving, when he'd return and do some serious deer hunting with Hawk. But it wasn't working. As a matter of fact, it was making matters worse.

"You're going to think I'm crazy," he finally said. "But I guess I'm still wound up from handing in the final paper I've worked on all summer, and I've got a vicious headache. Could I just go home?"

"But that's supposed to be my line when I'm

bored with a date.'' She giggled impishly. ''Parker, you aren't bored with me, are you?''

He looked right into her blue eyes, his own blinking back a fake headache, and lied through his teeth just like he did the day Creole asked him what color his truck was. ''Of course not, darling. Just drive me back to your place and I'll take this tired old hunk of bones home and sleep a week. That paper sure took a lot out of me.''

''I can see that. You look like warmed over sin on Sunday morning. Come on, sweetheart. We'll do this again later when you've got more energy.'' She took him by the hand, flipped a bill on the table, shushed him when he protested and led him out of the restaurant.

''Sure you don't want to come inside and curl up beside me for the night? I'll rub your temples and make the poor little baby forget all about that demanding old computer and all those words.'' She kissed his fingertips as he got out of the car.

''No thanks. I'd be horrible company. I'll just pull the blinds and sleep for a week in my own bed. It's calling my name right now. Sorry about the evening, Vickey.'' He kissed her on the cheek, but lights didn't go off and bells didn't ring—not like they did this morning when his lips touched Creole Hawk's forehead.

* * *

Creole put the sunglasses down on the vanity in her bathroom and looked in the mirror. The same dark-haired girl looked back at her as when she'd left home for her last day at the college. She promised Kyle she'd help him grade papers that day since she was free for a few days. And at the end of the day, he'd walked her to her car, kissed her goodbye and waved as she drove away. She thought her future was secure, and that someday, in the very near future the two of them would be planning a nice honeymoon.

"Boy, was I wrong!" she told her reflection. "One semi truck and my whole world took a one hundred eighty degree turn." She leaned forward, blinked several times and looked for any visible scars.

"Looks the same, Lady Creole." She used the same sarcastic voice Mr. Parker used when he addressed her like that. "Except that I've never laid eyes on the person who helped me grow up. But someone on this ranch must know where he's from. And if the mountain won't come to Muhammad, then Muhammad might just have to find her way to the mountain. He might tell me to get lost and never bother him again, but by golly, at least I wouldn't have a blank where his face is supposed to be in my memory."

She leaned back, picked up her hairbrush and

attacked her long black hair. "That's exactly what I'll do. I shall begin with Julia tomorrow morning at breakfast and work my way through every cow-poke on this ranch if I have to." She smiled brightly, her green eyes twinkling in the mirror as she began to hum the Cajun love ballad. "I don't care if he's a pauper living in a tar paper shanty," she told the girl in the mirror. "I probably won't even like him when I meet him face to face. As big as his ego is and as violent as my temper is, we could never ever get along, but at least I'll know for sure, and I can get on with my life."

She sang at the top of her lungs in the shower, wrapped herself in an oversized towel, put her sun-glasses back on and flipped on CMT. Garth Brooks was singing a song about missing the dance. "Well, I didn't miss the dance," she muttered. "I had to provide the music and insist on him holding me, but I did have the dance. And now I'll meet the man. . . ."

Chapter Eight

Billy Hawk drew his black eyebrows down so tightly that the two brows became one solid line and his ebony eyes were mere slits. He could have accepted Creole saying she was going to take a year off and tour the world. But there she stood before him wearing faded denim jeans, a chambray shirt and work boots, declaring she was going to work cattle this morning and tomorrow she was going to drive a tractor and rake the hay he had down in the back pasture.

"But, Creole, you just got your bandages off, and—" he attempted to argue, knowing full well he'd just as argue with a stop sign. When Creole set her mind a whole band of angels couldn't make her change it. She was truly both her parents' child.

The Cajun stubborness mixed with the Cherokee determination surely made for a person who didn't take no for an answer.

''I've had six weeks to think about this. I'm going to work every morning with you at whatever you're doing. Just point me in the direction of what you need. And the afternoons I'm going to hole up in the den, Daddy. I've got the best education your money could buy and I'm taking over the bookkeeping. A new computer is arriving this afternoon, and I'm setting up shop. I'd use my personal computer in my bedroom but it doesn't have the memory to do what I intend to take care of. I called your accountant and he's sending over the disks with all your accounts today. I've already got the books out with the cattle records, and I'm going to start putting the information into the computer. By this time next month, I can push a button and we'll know the lineage of any bull on the ranch, who his grandpa was and how many calves he sired. Hawk Ridge will be mine someday, Daddy, and I'll not have somebody else running it for me.''

''But you're . . .'' He shook his head.

''A woman. That's right. And this is a new world we live in. Women fly in space. They are doctors and lawyers, and this one is going to be the best rancher since Billy Hawk.'' She smiled, and his heart melted. If she wanted to be a rancher, he'd

put her through the worst, longest, hardest training
he could manage. If she lasted past Thanksgiving
when she was going to Louisiana for the holidays,
he'd eat his hat and have his work boots for dessert.
He'd break his spoiled daughter, and her training
would begin this very morning. By the time he got
finished with her, she'd be begging for a vacation
on an island where no cows or tractors could be
found. She'll be wanting to shop for fancy dresses
and looking for a husband who wears white shirts
and doesn't know the back end of a brood sow
from a hay hook.

"Okay. If that's what you want." He nodded.
"Saddle up Highness and ride out to the back pasture land with Slim. Bring in all the strays, so Hank
and I can vaccinate and work them today. When
we break for noon, you can start your office work
in the den, but I want you on the tractor as soon
as day breaks tomorrow morning. The day after that
I can use you on the bailer. Slim can throw the
bails on the back of the truck, but you can use a
pair of hooks and help him stack those square bails
in the barn. And I like the idea of putting all the
records into the computer. I'll expect some kind of
spreadsheet on Friday evening at four o'clock each
week."

"Yes, sir," she said.

"And, Creole, if you have a change of heart or

anytime the going gets too tough, you can back out of this deal,'' he said.

"When the going gets tough, the tough get going.'' She threw her head back as she cleared the living room in a few long, easy strides. "That's a Billy Hawk saying. And, Daddy, remember I'm part Cajun and part Cherokee. I expect that makes some pretty tough genes. See you at lunch time. Tell Julia she better put on an extra pound of beans and barbecue another rack of ribs, because after I round up cattle all morning, I'm going to be ready to eat a steer—hoof, horns, and even the bellow.''

The sweet aroma of fresh baked yeast bread greeted her when she opened the back door. She shucked her dirty work boots at the back door and rubbed her sore hips. She and Slim had put in a hard morning, but every bovine had been rounded up. Not even that deranged yearling hiding behind the scrub oak had outsmarted her and her horse, Highness, who was delighted to be out of the barn and running again.

"Julia, this house smells wonderful,'' she declared, moaning as she watched the cook take a blackberry cobbler from the oven. She washed her hands in the kitchen sink and grabbed a stack of plates from the cabinets. "How many are we setting?''

"Five," Julia said. "Billy, Hank, Slim, you and me. The rest of them took the chuck wagon and Ben to cook for them. They didn't want to waste time coming back in for dinner. So, how'd your first day go?"

"Fast," she laughed.

"Bunch of men brought in some big boxes. Said they were supposed to set them in the den." Julia heaped candied sweet potatoes and poured up steaming hot baked beans in crock bowls.

"That's right. That's the afternoon job. Daddy says I can work like a field hand in the mornings. But in the afternoons, I'm going to run the business end of this deal. Between the two, I expect I'll stay busy enough to stay out of trouble." She grabbed a hot roll and bit into it.

"Leave that alone. You're going to ruin your dinner." Julia slapped her hand good-naturedly. She was glad to see this spoiled child take the reins in her hands and begin to show a little responsibility. She'd known the day would come—eventually. After all, Billy had spoiled her, but he'd taught her a few things along the way. But when Billy told her this morning that Creole had gone for a long walk last night and this morning declared she was going to start to work, she was still surprised.

"Not with one little roll," Creole said. "It'd take

at least half a side of beef to ruin my dinner today. I hear the men coming. Let's get the food on the table so Daddy can grace it and we can eat.''

After dinner, Julia chased the three men into the den and served them strong, hot, black coffee while she cleaned off the table. She expected Creole to dive right into the boxes and set up her equipment, but instead she helped Julia clear the table and load the dishwasher. ''You better get in there and get into that computer stuff,'' Julia told her.

''When they clear out.'' Creole hummed under her breath. ''They'll get in my way,'' she said. ''Tell me something, Julia. Where did Mr. Parker come from?''

Julia almost dropped the last two glasses she carried from the table. ''Why?'' she asked, buying a little time to collect her scattered thoughts into a reasonable answer.

''Well, he dropped in here out of nowhere and then disappeared. It was like he was just a voice and a robot to lead me around,'' Creole said as nonchalantly as possible, trying to keep her tone cool and uncaring.

''Didn't act like no robot to me,'' Julia snorted. ''Seems like he kept you mad enough to eat railroad spikes most of the time. Seems like I remember one day you said if he crossed you one more time, as soon as you got your eyesight back you

was going to shoot him dead. Maybe he overheard
you say that and decided to get out of Hawk Ridge
while the getting was good.''

''You didn't answer me.'' Creole leaned against
the bar, crossed her arms over her chest and waited.
''Where did he come from?''

''Who knows?'' Julia shrugged. ''Probably from
heaven. Like that television show where an angel
goes around doing things to help people. Mr. Parker just drove up out there in that new truck and
asked your Daddy for the job of caring for you.
And he just drove away when the job was done.''

''In other words, you're not saying anything,''
Creole chuckled. Julia's pursed lips said volumes
more than the words she spoke. She knew Mr. Parker, who he was, where he came from and where
he went. And if Creole just watched her, Julia
would eventually drop a hint.

''You got that right, my child. Now go work as
hard on that machinery as you worked this morning
in the pasture, and I'll see to it you get a decent
supper.'' She turned her back, glad the conversation was over. She'd have to be careful what she
said or Creole would be pressuring her for information again. She figured Creole would be so glad
to be rid of Johnny Rollin—or Mr. Parker, as he
called himself while he was here—that she'd be

dancing a jig and chasing off with Andrea to shop for a new truck.

When Billy and Hank came in at six o'clock for supper, they found Creole still wearing her chambray shirt and jeans, staring at the computer screen. She'd claimed a corner of the enormous den, right in front of the floor to ceiling glass windows. Squirrels played on the ground on the other side of the glass panes, and before long pecans would be dropping from the ancient trees in the backyard. A wooden swing swayed in the Oklahoma breeze.

She'd reviewed the accounts, familiarized herself with the debits and credits, talked to the banker for an hour and was entering data about their cattle when Billy and Hank called from the kitchen to tell her it was supper time. She glanced at the clock. Five hours had elapsed, and it only seemed like ten or fifteen minutes. Her stomach growled, reminding her that she hadn't even stopped for an afternoon snack, and she still had at least three hours of work to do before she fell into bed tonight. She'd been right—lots of hard work would erase that faceless man from her thoughts.

''Make heads or tails out of the books?'' her father asked, passing a platter of corn on the cob to her.

''Sure. The accountant has been using a simple program. I can save the ranch the money you've been giving him. I got into the file cabinet and re-vamped it to make it easier for me to get into the records. I'm putting data in about the cattle now.'' She buttered the corn and bit into it, dripping butter down the front of her shirt. ''Oops,'' she laughed. ''Not bad manners, just good corn,'' she said. ''So what did you two do all afternoon? Lay out in the hay and take a nap, then come dragging in here trying to convince me and Julia you worked hard?'' she teased.

''You think so,'' Hank said, and she heard the same inflection Mr. Parker used when he said that same thing to her more than once. Strange that he would have the same voice as Mr. Parker, but maybe it was just her imagination playing tricks on her. ''I'll have you know, young lady,'' he poked his fork at her as he spoke, ''that we really worked this afternoon since we didn't have to wait on a slow old girl to get her job done before we could do ours.''

''Oh, hush,'' she snipped. ''You wouldn't be able to walk in that back door if you worked that hard. And one other thing, Hank. Tell me about Mr. Parker while we're eating.''

''What?'' His big old brown eyes widened until she thought they'd pop right out of his head. Her father covered his mouth with a napkin as he coughed, and she knew beyond a shadow of a doubt that she'd stepped on a sore spot with both of them. Well, they could just cough up the evidence she wanted, or else she'd make them uncomfortable every day.

"He was here all those weeks and then just disappeared. I suppose you all got to know him pretty well during that time." She continued to eat her way around the corn as she talked. "He was too stubborn to stay just one more day so I could actually see what he looked like, so my curiosity is piqued. What did he look like?"

Hank's tongue was stuck to the roof of his mouth so tightly he couldn't say a word for several minutes. He swallowed several times and caught Julia fighting back a bad case of giggles. So the imp had already put Julia on the spot. She could have at least told him and Billy that Creole was asking questions. If she wasn't such a good cook and Slim's wife, he'd beg Billy to fire her on the spot.

"Well?" Creole pressured.

"I don't know." Hank stumbled over the words. "He was medium height I guess, wasn't he, Billy?"

"Oh, about your height I guess," Billy said, not giving him an ounce of help.

"What color was his hair?" Creole asked.

"Oh, brown or—"

"Black," Billy said. "It was black, kind of like Creole's hair. Only he didn't wear it as long as she does. I wouldn't hire a man with a ponytail. Not to herd my cattle—or even put up with my daughter's sass."

Hank sighed in relief. Billy was going to help him after all. Between the two of them, they could build a picture she'd accept, then forget. "Kind of muscular, wouldn't you say, Billy?"

"Oh, yes, I wouldn't want a weak man taking care of Creole. She's a big girl you know. What if she stumbled over a rock and fell and he couldn't even pick her up? I thought he was going to have to do just that when she wouldn't get in the pickup truck," Billy said seriously.

"You're both talking about me like I'm not here," she huffed. "Evidently you're hiding something because you're talking in circles. So I won't ask you anything else. Just forget it. I don't care anyway. He was egotistical and about all he did was make me mad every day. Just forget I even asked."

Late that night, she threw back her neck and rolled it back and forth, trying to get the kinks out of the muscles, tired from staring at a computer screen all afternoon and evening. A walk was just what she needed. Then she'd be so tired, sleep would jump out of the darkness, and before she knew it, the alarm would be going off, telling her to get up.

She shoved her feet down into a pair of worn sneakers. She opened the door, inhaled the fresh night air and shut her eyes. Yes, there were the frogs and crickets doing a repeat performance from last night. Glory, the blue heeler, rounded the corner of the house and waited. If she was going for a walk, then Glory full well intended to go with her. Somewhere along the way she might sit down and rub Glory's ears like she did last night, and the dog wasn't going to miss a chance like that.

Out of habit, she walked down the cattle trail toward the pond. But before she got to the next leg of what had become her morning walk with her caretaker, she turned right and followed the path back to Hank's cabin. At least they called it a cabin, and it might have started out as one in the beginning, but it was now a small ranch house with three bedrooms, a couple of bathrooms and a nice big great room, housing a kitchen, cozy living room and a dining area. She hadn't been inside the house for at least five years, but she saw lights burning brightly, and before she even realized what she was doing, she knocked on the door.

"Something wrong?" Hank's face showed concern.

"Nope, just out for a walk and saw your light.

Got a cup of coffee for a tired old girl?'' she asked.

''Sure, come on in, Creole,'' Hank said.

She stepped out of her shoes just inside the door, leaving them beside Hank's brown work boots. Nothing had changed since she was here the last time. A paperback Louis L'Amour book was turned upside down on Hank's chair arm. He had read all of the series at least a dozen times, and she couldn't remember a time when he wasn't reading one of them.

''Still a Louis fan, I see.'' She picked up the book, checking the title.

''Always will be. Tried some of that new stuff. But always go back to old Louis. Those folks in his books are my buddies.'' He handed her a cup of hot black coffee. ''Sit down a spell, Creole.''

She sunk back into the comfortable leather sofa and sipped the coffee. ''Just like you taught me to drink it. Black as tar and stiff enough to hold up a silver spoon,'' she laughed. ''Remember when I came over here when I was about twelve and wanted a cup of coffee?''

''Yep.'' Hank grinned broadly. ''After the first drink, you said you wanted some sugar and cream and I told you to drink coffee or drink milk shakes but not to mix the two. I think you just drank it out of pure spite.''

''I did,'' she said.

"Yep," Hank said. "What you out so late for, girl?"

"Just working the kinks out before I go to sleep," she said honestly, her eyes fixing on a familiar photograph on the mantle above the rock fireplace. Martha and Johnny on the front porch of the house. He was about five years old, and even then, he had that look on his face. That wide-eyed expression she hated. The one that felt sorry for her because his mother loved him more than her mother loved her.

But there was a new photo in a rough cedar frame right beside it. It was a grown man who looked a lot like Hank—all except for those odd eyes. He always did have those haunting eyes like his mother, and his face didn't have all the angles Hank's did. He'd grown up to be a fairly nice-looking man after all. But even from the picture, she could tell she wouldn't like him.

"New picture of Johnny, I see," she said.

Hank swallowed quickly to keep from spewing coffee across the carpet. Then he remembered that she'd never actually seen his son during the weeks he'd been on the ranch. "Yes, he had it made a few months ago. Sent it to me for Father's Day."

"Oh, I see." She glanced at it again. "Well, thanks for the coffee. I think I'm tired enough the caffeine won't even keep me awake. I'll see you at lunch tomorrow,'' she said.

''Where you been?'' her father asked from the shadows of the front porch, making her jump.

''You scared me,'' she said.

''Didn't mean to,'' he said. ''Out for a walk?''

''Yes, to work out some kinks. Stopped by Hank's for a cup of coffee. Hadn't been there in a long time. He's got a new picture of Johnny,'' she said.

Billy gasped and she caught the sound. ''Something wrong, Daddy?''

''No, just sighing. Tired I guess. What was that about a new picture?''

''One of Johnny, I said. Not a bad-looking man. Looks a lot like Hank. Got his mother's eyes though. I never did like that kid, you know. I'm glad I'm gone when he visits. I wouldn't like him now either,'' she said. ''I'm going to bed. Bet I don't have to count sheep tonight.'' She stopped and kissed Billy on the top of his head, something she hadn't done in years.

Chapter Nine

Billy Hawk kept Creole so busy she didn't know
what happened to the days, weeks or months, but
as tired as she was when her head hit the pillow at
night, she still dreamed of a faceless man who
made her blood boil and her heart race. She knew
it was Mr. Parker haunting her dreams, and she
attributed it all to the unknown. She had proved
she could withstand almost anything—except not
knowing what was going on. When her mother left,
she pouted and cried but there was no unknown.
Evangelina was gone and she wasn't coming back,
so although she was a hot-headed, spoiled little girl,
she'd come to grips with it. Blindness, just for six
weeks, had terrified her, but it did have an end so
she'd endured it.

But this mysterious obsession with Mr. Parker existed because there was an unknown involved. She couldn't stand not knowing who he was, what puff of wind carried him away and why she even still cared. She'd rode Highness around the fence lines this morning, tightening up any sagging barbed wire and making sure all the posts were steady before winter actually set in. She'd treated herself to a fast shower, pulled on a pair of gray sweat pants and a faded T-shirt, and tied her hair back with a red bandanna. She turned on the computer and picked up a stack of papers about those new cows Billy and Hank brought in yesterday from the cattle sale in Sulphur, Oklahoma, thirty miles south of Ada. From a quick glance at their pedigrees, it looked like they'd done pretty well at the sale. The phone on her desk rang, and she picked it up absent-mindedly, still reviewing the papers while she said, "Hello."

"Creole, this is Kyle," he said, as he had every day for the past two months.

"Yes?" she said curtly, putting the papers down.

"Thought you might like to take in a movie this week. Or maybe have Thanksgiving dinner with me at my folk's house. Are you going to Louisiana or are you free?" he asked with more confidence in his voice than she wanted to hear. So he wanted to pick up where they left off, did he? Well, he could wish in one hand and spit in the other and see which one filled up fastest.

"I cannot believe you're calling me, Kyle. What happened to the woman who made you feel like a king and who was going to be your perfect wife?"

"I don't need this from you, Creole. I happen to know you aren't seeing anyone, and things didn't work out with Amber, so I thought . . ."

"Well, that's where you made your first mistake, Kyle. You thought, and in order to think, a person must have two brain cells rubbing together, and you don't have that many active cells in your brain or else you would know better than to call me after the way you treated me when I was blind. No, I'm not interested in dinner with you or Thanksgiving dinner with your folks. I do not want to see you again—not now or ever, and I don't want to hear from you again, either." She took a sharp inhale to give him more of her mind on the matter, but a loud click in her ear stopped the tirade.

She laid the phone down and laughed. At least she'd had the last word with him after all. She hoped she'd scorched the hair out of his ears and all the stupid ideas out of his hollow head forever. If she never heard his name or his voice again it would be entirely too soon.

"Hey, you're supposed to be off the rest of the week. Thanksgiving is in two days, and your mother probably has your name engraved on a place card for the dinner table.'' Billy padded into the den in his socks. ''Looks like rain is going to run me and Hank inside for the afternoon. We could get out there in the horse barn and polish tack, but we're feeling lazy. Besides, we've got this new cow hand who's making our jobs around here easier,'' he grinned.

''Oh, and who's that?'' she teased.

''This good-looking chick who's proving her mettle. I believe she might be about to pass her probation period. I might even hire her full-time.'' Billy sat down in his overstuffed recliner. He picked up a remote control and turned on the television set to an afternoon talk show. ''So you flying down this year? Want me to take you to the airport tomorrow?''

''I'm not going this year.'' Creole didn't even look up from the papers. ''Too much work. Too little time. Some other sorry old cowpoke might move in on my territory and talk you into giving him my job, and I've worked too hard to let someone else take over my claim.''

Billy Hawk gasped. ''But you always go to your mother's for the holidays,'' he said.

''Don't want me around? Got a lady friend you only see when I'm out of the picture?'' she teased.

''Had several lady friends through the years, and

you've known about every one of them," he said. "Just wasn't expecting you to stay home. As you know it's not the big hoopla you're used to in the south. Just us and Hank . . . and Johnny Rollin."

She still didn't look up. So Johnny Rollin was coming for Thanksgiving. Well, hallelujah! That was just the frosting on the cake. Maybe he'd only be there for the day. She'd just have to be civil while they ate their turkey and he'd go back to Texas.

"Did you hear me, Creole? I said Johnny Rollin is coming for Thanksgiving. He'll be here from Tuesday night through Sunday. We're going to deer hunt on Wednesday and Thursday. Me and Hank and Slim and Johnny. Then we'll eat our Thanksgiving meal at supper time. There won't be a fancy party. . . . and Johnny always eats with us," Billy said, sure she'd reconsider and grab the phone to make the reservations on the next flight south out of Oklahoma City.

"I heard you, Daddy," she said. "I'm a big girl now, not a kid afraid Johnny is going to steal my place on this ranch. I probably won't like him any better than when I was a child, but there's relatives on my stepdad's side I don't like either, and so far I haven't spit in anyone's eye. That don't mean the idea hasn't crossed my mind more than once. I expect I can sit at the same table with Johnny and I betcha I can even be a lady.''

''I'll believe it when I see it.'' He rolled his eyes. ''I'll give you both days off. Wednesday and Thursday. You can call Andrea and have a day in town on Wednesday and entertain yourself on Thursday until we come home from deer hunting.''

''Well, thank you very much, kind sir.'' She giggled. ''And what if I want to go deer hunting with you?''

''Oh, no! That's where I draw the line,'' he stated bluntly.

''Hey, don't get so upset. I couldn't shoot Bambi's mother. Even if you did let me go, I'd probably scream for the deer to run about the time you raised the gun. How anyone can shoot one of those pretty creatures is a mystery to me.'' She laughed. ''Tell me something. Did Mr. Parker like to hunt?''

Billy rolled his eyes again. She'd tried to sneak in several questions about him these past weeks and he'd fended them all off without giving anything away. ''I didn't talk to Mr. Parker about hunting,'' he said honestly.

''Oh, what did you talk to him about?''

''You. He gave me a report each evening when he left and that's what I talked to Mr. Parker about,'' he said.

"Did you pay him with cash?"

"What on earth brought that on?" he asked.

"I've been through the accounts. There's not a single canceled check with his name on it, so you didn't pay him with checks. So did you give him cash? How much did it cost you for him to insult me every day, Daddy?"

"More than you'll ever know—and I'm not about to tell you what I paid that young man to keep you on your toes." He laughed. She'd never know that Mr. Parker and Johnny Rollin were one and the same. He could even sit across the table from him on Thanksgiving and Billy wouldn't give away the secret. The boy had been a pure godsend in his time of trouble, but he would never let Creole know Mr. Parker's real identity. He'd have to keep his eyes on his plate and not look at Hank during the meal, though. And heaven help them all if she asked one of her sly questions about Mr. Parker while Johnny was at the table. He'd probably choke to death on a bit of Julia's cornbread dressing, and he and Hank would get so tickled Creole would pitch a fit about them laughing at her.

"I guess you and Hank still think Johnny hung the moon and stars," she smarted off in the sassy tone Billy had begun to think was gone forever.

"Yep, and the sun comes up just to shine on him. He's one in a million. Wish you didn't hate

128 *Carolyn Brown*

him so badly. He's a fine young man,'' Billy intoned like a preacher delivering a sermon to a
church full of sinners.

''Oh, no, you don't.'' She jerked her head up.
''He might have wings and a halo, but I'll never,
ever like that man. He's insolent, and he was mean
to me when I was little.''

''Oh, and I was thinking about him for a son-in-
law,'' Billy teased.

''Well, you can stop thinking,'' Creole snorted.
''If Johnny Rollin was the last man on earth and I
was the very last woman, then the human species
would completely die out. I'm going to bed now.''
She blew him a kiss from the door, and wondered
what in the world tickled him so badly he had to
drag out his handkerchief and wipe the tears from
his eyes.

Parker removed his suitcase and gun case from
behind the seat in his pickup. He bumped the door-
bell but didn't wait on Hank to open the door. He
nosed his suitcase in the front door ahead of him
and had dropped it on the floor when Hank came
from a back bedroom. ''Been expecting you for an
hour.'' He gave his son a quick hug and helped
him carry his baggage to the bedroom, which had
been his since birth.

''Got caught in rush hour traffic out on I-35,''

Parker said. "I think there's a northern blowin' in from Kansas. Weatherman said to expect a heavy frost tomorrow morning. Ya'll ready to shoot a big buck?"

"A trophy." Hank nodded. "That's what I want this year. One I can hang on the wall above the mantel. At least fourteen points."

"Whew, you ain't wantin' much, are you, Dad?"

"Might as well wish big if that's all you get." Hank laughed. "Supper is waiting in the microwave. I made Julia fix you up a plate of barbecue brisket and some pintos. Then you better hit the sack, son. Got to get up early, you know."

"Yes, sir, a team of wild horses or a raging tornado couldn't keep me awake tonight. I'm so tired my old eyes will be shut before my head hits the pillow," Parker said.

"Oh, yeah, I guess I oughta warn you. When you left, Creole was so mad at you she was ready to send out the National Guard to find you. She was determined she was going to see your face, and she's asked a lot of questions, which we just avoided. She's about stopped, now." Hank rubbed his chin.

"She was pretty aggravated that last day," Parker said. "But there wasn't any way I could go to that doctor's appointment with her. Her blood pressure would have probably blinded her for life if she'd looked up and saw Johnny Rollin standing there beside her. And if she figured out it was me all those weeks, she'd come gunnin' for all of us,'' he laughed, but it was brittle.

''You're right. Anyway, she's not going to Louisiana for the holiday. She's at the ranch, so you'll have to sit at the Thanksgiving supper with her. And you'll have to watch your step, son. I hate to tell you that. Guess I could have called and let you decide whether you wanted to come on up here, but pure old selfishness kept me from doing it. I wanted to spend some time with you, and I figured you was smart enough to—''

''It's all right, Dad. Mr. Parker is gone. And Johnny Rollin never did appeal to that girl. She'd dance a jig on my grave,'' he said. ''Now, where's that barbecue? I'm just a split second away from pure starvation.''

Parker couldn't sleep when his head hit the pillow. He tossed and turned, thought about Creole even when he didn't want to, fluffed his pillow a dozen times, and finally crawled out of bed, got dressed and went out for a walk. Perhaps the norther would blow in and he'd be thankful for a nice warm bed to curl up in. He noticed the light was on in her bedroom when he rounded the ranch house. So she was still awake, too. Probably talking to her newest boyfriend—or Andrea—on the phone. Hank told him that she and Andrea would be out tomorrow. She was actually going into town to look at a truck.

He was surprised she hadn't bought something before now, but Hank said she'd tied herself to the ranch and only left on Sundays, when she accompanied him and Billy to church. Any other day, she was up at dawn and hard at work until noon, when she took the same hour off they did, then she was in the den until dark doing business. She'd gotten the top dollar for their excess hay this year, and she had sold off the old stock and made them replace several cows with new ones. Hank had sung her praises until Parker's ears hurt as much as his pride.

He listened to the frogs and crickets. It might be the last night they sang their mournful tunes if the frost that the weatherman ordered did materialize. Glory nosed his hand, practically scaring the liver right out of him. ''You silly old girl.'' He scratched her ears. ''Where did you come from?''

Glory had just walked back to the house with Creole and was coming toward her dog house when she saw the man strolling out toward the pond. Humans sure were strange creatures. If he'd hurried up a little bit, he could have walked with Creole like they did in the summer. But Glory was just a dog, and she couldn't tell human beings how to run their business.

Strange, but Parker could swear he caught a whiff of Creole's perfume. He turned quickly to see if she was out for a late night walk, but he only saw the yellow glow of the light filtering through her bedroom window. He sat down in the brittle grass and wondered what she'd do if he walked down the hallway right then, opened her door and said, "Hello, Creole." Would she see Johnny Rollin before her, or would she use all those senses he helped her discover and hear Mr. Parker?

He had no answer to his question. He slowly made his way back to his father's house. At least he was tired enough to sleep, even if fitfully, until the alarm went off and Hank knocked on the door. "Huntin' season commences in one hour. Breakfast is ready," he called excitedly.

Creole heard the truck as it passed the house and drove down the lane toward Hank's place. So Johnny had arrived, and he drove a truck these days. She expected him to float in on a white cloud with angels blowing trumpets before him and Gabriel, himself, bringing up the rear. What was it Julia said about Mr. Parker? He was like that show on television about the human angel who went around doing good things. Maybe they used Johnny

Rollin for the role model and Mr. Parker was just one of his protégés.

She saw the truck parked beside Hank's house when she went out for what had become her ritual evening walk, but tonight she didn't stop by Hank's for coffee. Thanksgiving dinner would tax her tolerance. She sure didn't want to spend any extra time around that particular man. Fifteen minutes and her own crooked halo would fall completely off.

She slept poorly, dreaming again about a faceless man with Martha Rollin's eyes, but at least when she awoke the great white hunters had already hit the woods, hunting the biggest trophy deer in all of the state. Probably what they'd bring home was a case of chiggers and ticks and stories about how the buck only slightly smaller than an Angus bull ran off into the woods with six pounds of lead in his shoulder. They'd talk about the hunt for weeks. And there would be four of them instead of just Hank, Billy and Slim. Of course, Johnny was probably hunting with golden bullets poured up for him by Saint Peter himself.

At nine o'clock, Andrea picked her up to take her to shop for a new truck. She honked, and Creole finished her juice, grabbed her purse and yelled at Julia that she would be home after lunch.

"Hey, where is he?" Andrea was flushed with excitement.

"Who?" Creole raised an eyebrow.

"Mr. Parker. That's his truck back there by Hank's house," Andrea giggled. "Don't you try to hide it from me, girlfriend. I saw that truck when he brought you to church and when I came out here to see you all those times."

"That's Johnny Rollin's truck. It might be the same color as Mr. Parker's, but it's not him. Trust me. I've got to put up with the wonderful Johnny for Thanksgiving supper." She rolled her eyes toward the sky. "Take me to buy a truck, Andrea, and if I look at a red one, shoot me."

By ten, she'd picked out a rich cranberry red truck with chrome running boards and a gray velvet interior. Andrea laughed at her when she said she wasn't going to let Mr. Parker, Johnny Rollin or fear talk her out of that beautiful piece of machinery. She considered a small truck like she'd driven for years, but like the cushy way Mr. Parker's truck rode and opted for a full-sized one. They started their Christmas shopping a couple of days early and had lunch at a Bandana's. Then Andrea had to go to her in-laws to help with Thanksgiving decorations, and Creole drove her brand-new truck home, parked it in the driveway and curled up on the sofa with the newest Sue Grafton book, which she'd bought that day.

''So are we making turkey or ham?'' She wiped the sleep from her eyes as she poured herself a cup of coffee.

''Both,'' Julia said. ''Billy likes ham on Thanksgiving and Slim thinks he's got to have turkey. So I fix both and we'll eat leftovers all week.'' She opened the oven and shoved a couple of pumpkin pies inside. ''What are you up to all day?''

''Whatever you need me to do. I read a book in the afternoon and then picked up one of John Grisham's about an hour before bedtime and didn't finish it until the early hours.'' She grinned. ''I probably look like I've been up for three days.''

''Four,'' Julia laughed. ''But a shower and something other than faded gray sweat bottoms that are two—'' she stood back and looked at Creole's legs sticking out from the bottom of the pants, ''—no, four inches too short, will make you presentable. You don't have to dress in sequins and velvet, but something nicer than jeans and a chambray would be acceptable.''

''You mean I've got to dress up for Johnny?'' She set her jaw in a familiar old attitude.

''Nope, but it would be nice if you dressed up a little for Billy Hawk today. It's been a long time since you set up to the table for a holiday with your Daddy, Creole,'' Julia scolded.

''Yes, ma'am.'' She saluted smartly. ''I shall wear my diamond tiara and be the princess today. Now let me make the cranberry salad and pecan pies. I'll die of boredom if I don't help,'' she said.

''Well, I don't turn down good help,'' Julia said.

At six o'clock, Billy Hawk came through the front door. Candles were burning on the dining room table, which was covered with a lace cloth and set with the best crystal and china in the house. A fresh bouquet of wildflowers was arranged in a silver vase in the middle of the table. Creole was dressed in a long dress of some kind of red silky material. It had gold buttons on the shoulders and a slit up the side. If Johnny Rollin didn't fall all over himself when he saw her, then Billy Hawk was taking him to town tomorrow and having *his* eyes checked.

''Hi, Daddy,'' Creole said as she placed white linen napkins at each place setting. ''How does it look? Even place cards . . . if you'll notice.'' She winked.

''My, oh my. How much will it cost me for you to stay home every year? You look like something out of a magazine. I better take a quick shower and get dressed. This sweaty old hunter can't set up to a table like that in this garb.'' He shook his head in amazement. ''That your new truck out there? I like the color. Darker red and bigger than what you had. 'Bout time you bought a real truck instead of a baby one.''

''Yep,'' she said. ''Dinner will be served promptly at six-thirty. So you better get a rush on it. Should I call Hank so he won't be late?''

''You better.'' He unbuttoned his shirt as he took off down the hallway.

The door opened at six-twenty-five, and Hank, with Johnny right behind him, came into the living room, which was dark except for hurricane lamps on the end tables. The dining room candles beckoned, and she could almost see Hank's eyes twinkle in the flickering lamp and candle lights.

''Hello, Creole.'' Johnny extended his hand.

''Johnny.'' She shook his hand amazed at the electrical jolt practically gluing her to the floor. *Now, where did that come from?* She asked herself. Crazy floor must have static electricity, and his black eel boots must have leather soles and be brand new.

Parker almost jerked his hand away from hers when they touched. It was the same hot sensation he got when he kissed her on the forehead that last day, but evidently she didn't feel it because she just stood there like she could easily feed him to the coyotes for supper. "It's been a long time," he said.

"Yes, it has." She shut her eyes for just a minute, trying to figure out what it was that tickled her soul. She thought she'd heard that voice before— lots of times. But that was silly. The last time she heard Johnny Rollin, he still had a high squeaky little boy's voice. "Well are we ready to sit down? Julia and I've worked all day on this meal so you better all make some appreciative noises."

She arranged the place cards so that Johnny sat across the table from her rather than beside her. Better to look up and see him, than to bump elbows with him. He'd grown up to be quite a handsome man. His jeans were creased and bunched up around the tops of his boots perfectly. The white western shirt was starched to perfection, which made her remember the day Mr. Parker took her to dinner at the Citgo station and said he'd probably drop chili on his starched white shirt. Well, Johnny was much too perfect to drop even a speck of giblet gravy on his shirt.

"Mmmm," he said. "Wonderful ham. Julia, this is the best cranberry salad I've ever tasted."

"Creole made it." She smiled and winked quickly before Creole looked up from her plate. "She also made the pecan pies. She's a good cook when you can talk her into staying in the house and off the tractors and horses.''

''Hush,'' Creole laughed. ''Johnny isn't interested in what I do. But thank you for the compliment,'' she said, cooking her head one side. His eyes looked even more strange as an adult than they did as a child. That misty gray color like a winter sky right after a storm . . . just like his mother's eyes. *Strange, like spit colored*, she remembered Andrea telling her on the phone. *Like the sky . . .*

A streak of lightening snapped outside the dining room window, followed by a clap of thunder that practically caused Creole to dive under the table. ''Whew, where did that come from?'' She shivered, forgetting all about Johnny's weird eyes.

Johnny smiled. He thought the only things in the world she was afraid of were big black spiders. ''Guess the norther we were supposed to get last night is a day late. Betcha it's ten degrees colder out there right now,'' he said.

''Glad I got that buck today. Freeze my toenails off in the morning sitting up there in that tree stand tomorrow morning,'' Hank said.

The rain poured in sheets, and the electricity went off during supper, so it was a good thing they were eating by candlelight. Talk turned to the great deer hunt and the trophy Hank had really shot that evening, just before they came home. A strange little feeling kept biting at Creole, and she couldn't begin to understand where it came from.

For the first time she didn't want to murder Johnny Rollin, but rather found herself studying him when she was sure he wasn't looking. After dessert and coffee she excused herself for a minute to go to the bathroom, glad that she could find her way around the house without electricity. After all, she'd found she could maneuver quite well without light for several weeks.

She was coming down the hall when she heard him laugh. She stopped in her tracks. Mr. Parker had returned while she was in the bathroom. Her heart stopped for a minute and then a gush of anger fired it right back up. How dare he just walk in like he hadn't even been away and set down to her Thanksgiving table and laugh with the men?

"And then Dad yelled at me to hurry up and get there before the big old critter . . ." Johnny said, only it was Mr. Parker's voice talking. She shut her eyes tightly.

"I wonder what's taking Creole so long. Surely she didn't get lost in the dark," Julia said.

"Lady Creole. She could find her way out of the backside of a cave," he said. "She's got the sharpest senses you've ever seen."

And the answers to all her questions came with the next bolt of lightning. Johnny Rollin was Mr.

Parker! When the boom of thunder rocked the silence, she remembered . . . John Parker Rollin. Parker was his middle name—and that's what Martha called him most of the time.

Chapter Ten

She made her jelly-filled knees walk back to the table. She sat down and picked at her dessert, shutting her eyes while her head was dropped, listening to the men talk about the hunt. No matter how she tried to talk herself into believing Mr. Parker could not possibly be Johnny Rollin, the more she knew she was wrong. She took a deep breath and there was his woodsy after shave lotion floating across the turkey and the cold sweet potato casserole. If she could have touched his arm, she didn't have a doubt it would be the same one which led her around for five solid weeks.

But why? Good grief, he didn't like her one bit better than she did him, so why would he do that? Money? He had a wonderful job as a counselor in some medical place in Texas. What was it Hank said the last time she had coffee with him? Johnny was director of something at this exclusive little place where the rich and famous came to get rehabilitated when they drank too much or smoked too much. And that there was some facility in Ada begging him to take a supervisory position since he'd gotten his master's degree this summer.

"I'm very tired." She looked up to find Johnny staring right at her with those haunting eyes. "If Julia will excuse me from helping clean the table, I think I'll take something to ease this headache and go to bed."

What she wanted to do was throw all the expensive china and crystal off the table, crawl up in the middle of it and throw a stomping, childish fit. She wanted to tell them all she was in on the little secret, and she hoped they all got the job of shoveling coal in the devil's furnace for all eternity for their dirty trick. But most of all, she wanted to throw her heart out the window in the middle of the storm because it was fluttering around like it could fly when she looked across the table at Johnny Rollin.

"Sure." Billy waved from the end of the table. "And then there was this buck with a rack so big it wouldn't fit in a bushel basket, and I raised my gun very slowly." He picked up his arms and sighted down the barrel of an imaginary gun. "And boom, he ran towards the woods. I got another bead on him. This time, I let go with one that got him right in the heart and he kept running, and boom, another one . . .''

Parker watched her disappear down the hallway, his crazy heart trying to jump right out of his chest and go with her. But it was evident she'd had more than she could endure just sitting across the table from him for an hour. She sure wouldn't want to hear his footsteps coming down the dark hall, or hear his knock on her door. He listened with one ear to the story Billy was telling, smiling when he was supposed to, nodding occasionally, but what he heard was her bedroom door closing and somewhere in the far reaches of the big ranch house, a shower running.

Vicky told him he was crazy to come back to this backwater town for the holidays. She begged him to have the holiday meal with her family in Dallas. She'd even proposed to him last week. ''We can take a long honeymoon,'' she said. ''A six-month engagement. The biggest wedding in the whole state of Texas with a dozen bridesmaids and groomsmen, newspaper and magazine coverage. Paparazzi in helicopters and the whole nine yards. And then we can take a round-the-world cruise, and when we get home you can work in Daddy's firm. He can make a place for you. Everyone knows a big firm needs a psychologist. We'll pick out rings tomorrow, darling. I think I'd like something on a wide band." she held up her fingers imagining the glitter of a five carat diamond.

"Thanks, but no thanks," he told her, remembering the day Creole wanted him to have "the whole nine yards." He shook his head. "I love you, Vicky. You're my friend and I love you, but I don't like you."

"I don't like you either, darling. I don't even love you. But we make an awesome-looking couple, and if it don't work out, you can kick any bush between here and the Pacific Ocean and a dozen divorce lawyers will come running out. We'll have one of those friendly divorces and remain wonderful friends," she told him.

"Still, no thanks," he laughed good-heartedly. "I want to feel electrical jolts when I kiss the woman I marry. I want the marriage to last forever. I want her to hold my hand when I'm old and gray. I want her face to be the last thing I see and her voice to be the last thing I hear. And I want her to say, 'Don't walk too fast, honey. I'll catch up real soon, I promise.' And I want to spend eternity with her."

Vicky laughed until tears rolled down her cheeks. "If that's not the most ridiculous thing I've ever heard. That might have happened a hundred years ago in a dime store romance book, but this is the real world, Parker Rollin. If a marriage lasts more than a year, it's a pure miracle. Well, if you don't want to marry me, then I'll ask Tyler. He's been hanging on my coattails all summer. He won't be as handsome in the wedding pictures as you would have been, but he'll do.''

''Thanks, I guess,'' he said.

''And then Billy said, 'Hey come on down out of that tree and help me skin this big rascal,' '' Hank was saying as Parker shook thoughts of Vicky from his mind and came back to the conversation around the table.

''Excuse me.'' He laid his napkin on the table. ''The storm has stopped, and I think I'll go out on the porch and smell the fresh air. I don't get to see the stars as bright as they are right now. He motioned toward the window where the stars were so close he could have reached out and gathered a handful. ''Wonderful meal, Miss Julia. You haven't lost your touch,'' he patted her on the shoulder as he passed her chair.

''Well.'' Billy eyed Hank, Julia and Slim. ''Did I miss something? Did she ask a question and we didn't get it fielded right?''

''Nope,'' Hank said. ''I think they just purely don't like each other's company.''

Creole wrapped a big white towel around her

body and sat down in her recliner. It was as almost as dark in her room as it was all those weeks. All except for those beautiful, bright stars peeking through her window. She couldn't sort out the mixed emotions trembling inside her. One part was angry beyond words—and a speechless Cajun was as rare as any endangered species. The other part was relieved to at least know the identity of the man whom she'd shared all her secrets with those many weeks.

''Good grief. I told him how obstinate Johnny Rollin was and how much I hated him.'' She had to smile at that memory. It certainly took a big man to sit there and let her tell the story of his parents' marriage and divorce, when he could have told the story even better than she did.

She paced the floor, not needing to feel her way around the furniture. She opened a drawer and pulled out underwear, another drawer and found an oversized sweatshirt and groped around in her closet until her hands fell on a pair of jeans. When she was fully dressed, she shoved her feet into socks and shoes. She needed room to think and a long walk down the cow path might clear her mind.

Parker sat down in the porch swing, gave himself a shove and hoped the swaying motion would make him stop thinking. It didn't. He was going to have to tell her who he was while he was at Hawk Ridge.

That was all there was to it, and whether she liked it or not, they'd cross that bridge when the time came.

During the course of daylight to dark, five days a week, his stupid heart had fallen for that hot-headed, willful Cajun-Cherokee mix, and until he got her out of his mind, he wasn't worth a dime to anyone or anything. The storm that just shut down the electricity would be a tempest in a teacup compared to what she was going to say when she found out her arch enemy knew her secrets. One thing for sure, she'd probably pitch his heart out in the gravel and jump up and down on it when he told her how he felt.

Why, oh why did his heart do this to him anyway? No one could live for more than a few minutes without a heart, and yet, the crazy thing hadn't even consulted him when it decided to fall in love with the very worst choice it could have ever made. He smiled weakly at the notion of offering her a red plastic heart and watching her break it into a million pieces, then laugh at him while he tried to pick up the chunks and shove them back in his chest.

It wouldn't be that bad, but it wouldn't be far short of it. One thing for sure, he wasn't going to get anything settled sitting in the cold while the north wind blew across his face. Glory cold-nosed his finger tips, and he jumped. "Good grief, feller, you're a sly old guy, sneaking up on a man like that." He rubbed the dog's ears. "Might as well join me for a walk. We might figure something out if we walk far enough." He stood up, and Glory looked back at the house. Creole was coming down the hall. Glory could hear her and if the man waited just a minute they could all three take a walk together. But the man was already off the porch, taking long strides toward the pond. People sure were strange critters. Even stranger than those stupid cats who lived in the barn.

Creole grabbed a jacket from the coat closet. "I'm out for a walk," she called into the dining room where the party seemed to be breaking up. She noticed that Johnny was gone. Probably went back to his father's house to laugh at how they'd all duped her while she was blind. That was fine with her. She might just fly down to Louisiana on the next flight out of Oklahoma City and not come back until he was gone.

Her heart twitched and she wanted to slap fire out of it. How dare the crazy old thing let that abominable man sneak inside her soul? She would have never fallen for him in a million years if she'd known who he was. Mr. Parker . . . that's who helped her use her other senses to see. The psychologist who probably used her for a guinea pig for one of his projects. She'd been no more than a big hard-shelled June bug under a microscope and her stupid heart didn't have eyes or ears to know any better than to fall for his pretenses.

''Tell me what you smell,'' she murmured his words, then remembered the sound of the paper so many times. He'd been writing! It was the flutter of paper she heard, not the wind in the leaves. So she was right. Now, what did she do with this ache in her chest? He'd probably just look at her pitifully, like he did when they were children, if she told him how many times she'd thought of him these past weeks since he left. She'd even told him about how she hated him because his mother loved him enough to take him with her and her mother left her behind.

''What a mess.'' She shook her head, looking down at the pathway as she walked. Where was Glory? Usually that smart dog knew when she went out the front door and was right behind her. ''Guess he's taken up homestead on the back porch waiting for Julia to toss out the turkey leftovers for him.'' Creole giggled but it was hollow.

She stopped at the edge of the pond, standing in the shadows of the willow trees at the edge of the water. She was not going to her mother's house. She was going to confront Johnny and tell him she knew who he was and that she sure didn't appreciate being his research subject. And then she intended to tell him exactly how she felt, how that just the sound of his voice made her jittery, and the kiss he planted on her forehead still burned when she thought about it. If he looked at her with those attractive eyes and told her she was just infatuated with him because he helped her, then at least she'd know where she stood with the man. She could give her heart the dressing down it deserved for falling for the most unsuitable man in the whole universe, and get on with her life. This wasn't the first disappointment she'd ever had in life, and it sure wouldn't be the last—even if it probably was the biggest.

He was on the far side of the pond, standing in the shadows with his back to Creole. The path in front of him led straight ahead toward the front of the ranch, then it cut back around to the back of the house, and from there he was just a stone's throw to Hank's place. At least his mind was clear. Tomorrow morning at daybreak, before she had time to saddle up Highness or crawl into a tractor seat, he was going down the hallway to her bedroom door and tell her who he was and what had happened in the five weeks he spent with her. Whether she tossed him out on his ear or not would have a direct bearing on whether he went to the interview in Ada.

Hank was ecstatic that his son would be living with him again on Hawk Ridge, but if Creole proved to be the high-strung, spoiled woman Johnny figured she was since she'd gotten her sight back, then he could always rent an apartment in Ada. At least he could see his father often, even if he didn't live right on the ranch.

Glory could smell the woman and with his night vision he knew the lady waited on the other side of the pond for the man. But he started down the other path instead of walking back the same way he came. Glory looked at his back, and then at the woman who hugged herself, shivering in the cold. Finally, Glory growled down deep in his throat and the man stopped, looked back and cocked his head off to one side.

"What's the matter, fellow?" he asked softly. "Snake?"

Glory growled again, snarling his lips back until he showed his teeth. "What is it?" Parker lowered his voice to a whisper. The dog had always been friendly, had even stayed beside him all the way down the path and around the pond. He reached out to touch Glory's ears, and the dog barked several times. "It's all right, old man, it's me. I didn't change. It's Parker." He drew his hand back.

Creole heard the dog growl across the pond and

strained her eyes to see what was going on over there. Then she thought she heard a male voice. Instinctively she shut her eyes and listened harder. His voice carried over the moon and stars reflected in the pond water and she heard him say, "It's me . . . it's Parker."

Proof!

She stepped out of the shadows and onto the bank of the pond and started around it, walking slowing and gingerly in the wet dirt. All she needed was to slip and fall into the pond. Wouldn't Johnny Rollin die a thousand deaths if he had to rescue her out of the murky water and ruin his white shirt?

Parker looked back down the path where Glory had started running toward someone. He turned around, crossed his arms over his chest and watched a woman approach. There wasn't any doubt who it was Glory was chasing back to join Creole. Here came the blistering cussing. He wasn't going to have to wait until morning. He could just say, "Lady Creole," and she'd know.

She didn't stop until her nose was just inches from his. "John Parker Rollin," she whispered, icicles hanging on each word.

"Amanda Lady Creole Hawk," he said just as tartly.

"Why?"

"Because I was working on a thesis for my

master's degree and you were the perfect subject for it. Because I was here and Billy needed help, and because I wanted to do it,'' he said honestly, his soft gray eyes never leaving her face as he drank in every feature. If this starlit, bitterly cold night was all he ever had, then when he was an old man at least he would be able to go outside in the night air and conjure up her face again in his memory.

''For free?'' she asked.

''Well, it cost me a great deal.'' His eyes twinkled and the frost on her green eyes began to melt in spite of her anger.

''Oh?''

''Yes, it did.'' He wanted to reach out, take her in his arms and hold her forever. He wanted to tell her she was the one he'd fallen in love with, but fear of being pushed into the cold pond water kept him at bay. She'd do it in the blink of an eye and take Glory back to the house with her, leaving Parker on his own to crawl up that slimy embankment to safety.

''What exactly did it cost you?'' She bit her tongue to keep from smiling. She wanted to wrap her arms around his broad shoulders, bury her face in his chest and listen to his heart. But Johnny Rollin would probably push her away and laugh all the way back to Texas.

''It cost me my time—and I had to grow a new

tongue almost every day from biting the one in my mouth plumb off,'' he smarted off, and she fought down the temptation to kiss him.

''It cost me my pride,'' she said. ''When I figured out who you were and how you'd used me, I could have shot you.''

''And when did this great revelation fall out of heaven into your brain?'' he asked bluntly.

''Tonight. I tried to get them to tell me who you were, Johnny Rollin. I tried to catch them off guard so I could come and find you, Mr. Parker. I wanted to see you so the dreams would stop.'' She pushed her face so close to his he could feel the warmth of her breath.

''And what would you have done?''

''Probably would have used my Cajun blood to kill you and my Indian blood to hide you,'' she said.

''So what are we going to do now?'' he said.

''What happened to you in those five weeks?'' she asked without answering.

''I think probably the same thing that happened to you?'' he said honestly, hoping he wasn't reading that twinkle in her beautiful green eyes wrong. In front of him stood a woman, not a little girl who hated him for no legitimate reason. ''Want to know something? I hated you, too. Want to know why? Because you're daddy fought a legion of lawyers to keep you with him, and mine let my momma take me to Texas with her without a fight.''

''My daddy did what?'' Her eyes stopped twinkling and her heart skipped a beat.

''Didn't you know? He told your momma she could go marry her old love but she wasn't taking his daughter off Hawk Ridge. When she tried to get custody of you, he hired the best lawyers in the world, and by the time it was finished, she was lucky to get you for two weeks in the summer and a couple of holidays. I always envied you for that since I loved this ranch so much.''

''I didn't know,'' she murmured, battling tears hanging on her long black eyelashes.

''I know, but it's time you did,'' he said. ''It's time we grew up, Creole. I'm not the little boy who didn't like you and you're not the little girl who hated me. We're two grown adults now. And what do we intend to do about this situation we apparently got ourselves into this summer?''

''We'll worry about that later, Mr. Parker. Right now, I think I want to finish my walk and sleep on this before I say anything more. I won't kill you in your sleep, I promise. I trusted you. Now it's your turn. Trust me.'' She slipped her hand in his.

Chapter Eleven

Martha wrapped the parts to a food processor in pages from an old newspaper and put them in a cardboard box. She would miss Parker dropping by a couple of times a week for lunch, and Tory was already pitching a fit about him going back to that horrid ranch that claimed her brother for two weeks every summer of her life until he was a grown man.

"Son, this box is full," Martha called as he carried two suitcases of clothing downstairs to his truck. He'd sold his hide-a-bed sofa and given the rest of his furniture to a friend who was moving into an apartment for the first time, so all he had to take with him to Hawk Ridge were his kitchen items and clothing.

"That's the end of it," he yelled over his shoulder

at the door. "I'll get it in a minute, Mom."

She stood at the door, watching him with tears in her eyes. Parker looked just like Hank, walked like him, cocked his head off to the side just like him, and brooded silently when something bothered him, just like Hank. Hank Rollin stole her heart the first time she looked across the dance floor and saw him so straight and tall in his uniform. They were going to travel and see the world when he got the letter from Billy Hawk offering him a foreman's job on Hawk Ridge. She hated the ranch from the minute they left the two-lane highway and turned down the gravel lane, and six years later the hate had devoured most of the love she'd had for Hank. If she hadn't taken Parker back to civilization, she'd have withered up and died a bitter old woman. She loved Les, and Tory was a delight— but there was a piece of her heart that would always belong to Hank Rollin. And Parker was the light of her life.

"It's not easy for me to see you go back to that cursed place I hated so much," she said as he picked up the last box and they walked down the stairs together.

"But I never hated it, Mom." He hugged her tightly. "And it's where Creole is."

"I can't believe you'd ever fall for that kid. Not even a gold crown was good enough for her as a child, and I can't imagine her being any better as a grown woman. You aren't really entertaining ideas of a permanent commitment with her?'' Martha wanted to hear him laugh and tell her that was a long way down the road. He had a job to fit into right now and a move to get adjusted to.

''Creole does speak her mind.'' He hugged his mother a second time. ''Life won't be ho-hum with her, but yes, I'm entertaining the idea of marriage. I love her, mother. And I hope when you come to the wedding you'll forget about that little dark-haired girl and give her a chance. She's a hard worker and—''

''To think that even though I carried your young body out of there, your heart really did stay behind on Hawk Ridge. What did I do wrong?'' Martha asked.

''Not one thing, Mom,'' he said. ''I'll call next week. And if Creole says yes I'll give you enough time to buy a new dress.''

''Drive carefully and let me know about the new job,'' she said with a smile on her face to mask the tears in her heart.

''I'm not coming for Christmas, Mother,'' Creole said and waited.

''You didn't come for Thanksgiving, and now I won't see you at Christmas. You tell Billy Hawk it's down in writing that I get you for Christmas, and he better get ready for a—''

"Mother, I am twenty-three years old. Those custody papers ended when I was eighteen. Daddy doesn't even know I'm making this call. I'm not leaving Parker during the holidays. I want to spend Christmas Eve and Christmas with him. He's been gone two weeks and he's moving back to the ranch today, and I won't be separated from him again,'' she said.

"I can't believe after all I've done to encourage you to get away from that backwater existence that you'd say this to me.'' Creole could hear the pout in Evangelina's voice and imagine her dark eyes dancing in anger.

"Well, I did,'' Creole said shortly. "Parker should be here soon and I intend to spend every available minute with him. He'll have to work from eight to five every day except the holidays. I work on the ranch in the mornings and on business every afternoon, so we can see each other at the supper table and evenings. I won't give it up, Mother.''

"Little Johnny Rollin with those pale eyes. How could you ever fall in love with the hired hand's son, Creole? How could you be satisfied to live on a remote ranch when you could be the belle of all Louisiana if you just said the word? Let me send you on a round-the-world cruise. I can book you to leave tomorrow or next week. Call the tune and I'll make the travel agent dance to whatever you say. Think about this, Creole. You're too young to commit your life to Hawk Ridge.''

''My life is committed to Hawk Ridge, Mother. It's in my blood, and it's my home and someday it will belong to me by inheritance. Thanks for your concern, but I'm not a child and I don't need any more time to think about what I want,'' she said.

''You're not thinking about marriage anytime soon, are you?'' Evangelina shut her eyes and said a silent prayer, hoping her daughter would laugh and remind her that the hired hand's son had not even mentioned so lofty an idea.

''Yep, I am. If Parker doesn't propose to me by midnight on Christmas, then I'm going to force his hand. I'll propose to him if I have to. But don't worry, even though I'm getting married right here on Hawk Ridge, I'll give you at least a week's notice, and I won't expect you to stay in Oklahoma more than one day.'' She laughed.

Billy and Hank tossed hay off the back of a flat-bed truck to the cattle and filled the galvanized feeder with grain. Winter had arrived in Oklahoma on Thanksgiving night, and if the old timers and the sumac bushes were telling the truth, they'd be feeding through a long, bitter winter.

"So what do you think about our children?" Billy asked.

"Think they were made for each other," Hank answered. "Who would have thought that day when Martha took him away from me that I'd get him back someday? Guess things always work out in the end, don't they?"

"Guess so. I been scared out of my mind Creole would marry up with some fool like Kyle. Couldn't ask for no better than Johnny—or Parker, I guess we'll call him now." Billy smiled. "Reckon they'll just be content to eat supper together tonight, talk about what happened all day at the ranch and where he works, and then take one of those long walks together in the cold. Or maybe they'll tell us they're getting married next summer."

"Just think, Billy, we're going to see the next generation run this ranch, and our grandbabies are going to grow up right here." Hank rubbed his chin in thought. "Talk about getting a blessing out of a raw deal."

"Yep, and if your kid don't propose to mine by Christmas night, I'm going to take him aside and ask him what in the blue blazes is the matter. She's so in love with him, it's just plumb oozing out her pores. And every time he looks at her, I'm afraid he's going to eat her up." Billy tossed another bale off in the pasture.

"Well, if he hasn't taken care of matters by then, you'll have to stand in line behind me, old friend. I'm thinking a spring wedding might be nice. Maybe we'll make one of them gazebo things and set up the reception under the trees in the backyard."

"Sounds good to me. And maybe by the time we're fifty, we can at least have a little dark-haired grandson to play with," Billy said.

"Or a sassy little granddaughter just like Creole," Hank chuckled.

Parker combed back his dark hair and splashed on some of the cologne Creole liked. He picked up the velvet box he'd hidden in his briefcase the day before and put it in his coat pocket. Then he stacked the wrapped presents from under the cedar Christmas tree in the corner of the den, getting them ready to take to the ranch house for the festivities this evening. "You about ready?" he called down the hall to his father.

"Yep, I am," Hank checked his reflection in the mirror. Christmas Eve and the same man looked back at him who did a year ago, just before he and Johnny—Parker, mercy, but it was hard to teach an old new dog new tricks—went to the ranch house to exchange gifts with Billy, Julia and Slim. Only this year, Creole was there and the future looked brighter than it ever had before.

The phone rang just as Hank opened the door. "Hello." He juggled several presents in his arms as he answered it. "For you." He handed the receiver to Parker, who had to put his bundles down to take it.

"Yes?" he said.

"Merry Christmas, darling," Vicky said. "I just wanted you to be the first to know that Tyler and I are looking at rings. We're in the jewelry store right now," she giggled. "At least he is. I made an excuse to go to the bathroom, and he's waiting. I just wanted to give you one last chance before I actually let him buy my ring. One more chance, Parker, to live in civilization and see if we can defy those divorce statistics."

"No, thanks," he said with a chuckle, imagining Tyler sitting in a jewelry store waiting for Vicky. They'd make a wonderful couple. Both egotistical beyond measure. Both good-looking. It would be the wedding of the century in the whole state of Texas.

"Okay, just don't look back someday and wish you'd been a little more impulsive, darling. Good luck with your wilderness woman. And if statistics get you in the next year, come around. I might be tired of Tyler by then.'' She giggled again. ''Merry Christmas, you handsome old hunk.''

''Merry Christmas to you, Vicky. Good luck,'' he said as he hung up. ''Let's go,'' he said to Hank, picking up the brightly wrapped packages.

''You're here!'' Creole met them at the door, took the presents from Parker and put them under the tree. Then she turned, wrapped her long arms around his neck and pulled his mouth down to hers for a long kiss that caused electrical jolts all the way through his body.

''Whew,'' Hank cleared his throat. ''Been a long time since a good-looking woman kissed me like that,'' he said, and Billy nodded in agreement.

''Julia, they're here. Let's open presents.'' Creole didn't blush one bit, and kept one of her arms around his waist, hooking her fingers in a back belt loop of his jeans.

It was a flurry of paper and ribbons, and everyone held their breath when Creole picked up the last present, a long, skinny box wrapped in bright red foil paper and tied with a wide green satin bow. The shape wasn't right for a ring, but then maybe he'd had the jeweler put it in a different box to surprise her. She opened it slowly and flipped open the red velvet box to find a strand of pearls with a note saying that he would explain where she should wear them for the first time later that night, when they went for their evening walk.

She smiled brightly and shoved the note into the pocket of her dress, but when she looked up, there was a funeral-like shadow on Julia's and Slim's faces and the sadness in both Hank's and Billy's faces was enough to make her either giggle or weep. Evidently they'd been waiting for some big declaration of love in the way of an engagement ring. But Parker hadn't proposed to her yet and when he did, Creole surely hoped he didn't do it in front of the whole family. They'd share lots of time and events with Billy and Hank, as well as Julia and Slim, but she was glad she hadn't found a ring in the box.

As a matter of fact, since she'd talked to her mother, she'd begun to have second thoughts about this whole thing. What if she married Parker and in five years, his mother's blood surfaced and he hated Hawk Ridge? How could she watch him drive away from the ranch, knowing she'd never see him again? Hawk Ridge was home, security, the future. Maybe Evangelina had been right when she said Creole should wait a while to see if Parker could be content on the ranch.

But she didn't have to worry about that right now. They'd have eggnog, pumpkin bread spread with cream cheese, Julia's famous Oklahoma pecan candy, and they'd toast the first Christmas Eve Creole had spent with her father in a long, long time.

"You better grab a coat and your boots if we're going to take our nightly stroll," Parker said after they'd stuffed themselves.

"I think I'll change clothes." She smiled at up at him. "That north wind whipping up under this dress would probably freeze me to death. And if Glory cold-nosed my bare leg, I'd clear three counties, I'd jump so fast," she said. "Give me five minutes, Parker. I'll meet you on the porch if you want to round up Glory."

"Hey, son," Hank said once he heard her shut her bedroom door. "We was all kind of hoping you'd give her something other than a string of pearls."

"Oh?" Parker felt the grin tickling the corners of his mouth, the cleft in his chin deepening in amusement.

"Guess you know what I mean," Hank said.

"Yes, I do, but that's kind of private between me and Creole, isn't it, Dad? We won't keep it a secret when we make a decision like that, I promise," he said. "See ya'll later." He shoved his arms down his Sherpa-lined leather coat and disappeared out the door to wait for Creole.

She slipped on her own sheepskin-lined denim duster and waved at them just before she joined

Parker on the porch. She wrapped her arms around his neck again and felt the shock when their lips met. Would it always be like this, even when they were old and gray and the next generation or two were living on the ranch? She hoped so, and she hoped she could bury this niggling little doubt her mother had planted in her soul about Parker.

"Mmmmm." She snuggled down into his chest. "Now just exactly where am I supposed to wear that gorgeous piece of jewelry? I guess you didn't want me to ask right in front of the whole bunch of them, did you?"

"No, I didn't." He drew her close to his side, keeping his arm around her waist. Glory followed behind them as they stepped off the porch and headed down the trail toward the pond. This was the way it was supposed to work, just like in the beginning, according to the way Glory thought. They belonged together just like they did when Creole had those funny white things on her eyes and Parker led her around the pond every day.

Parker hoped she didn't feel his silly heart doing double time. She'd never given him any doubt that she wanted to spend the rest of her life with him, not once since that night four weeks ago when she slipped her hand in his and told him to trust her like she had trusted him. But proposing was serious business, and in spite of the fact that he had an impressive, well-paying job, she was still Creole Hawk and this whole ranch would be her inheritance someday. And there was always the possibility she would wake up one morning and feel like she'd married beneath her—and even his strong love wouldn't be able to hold their marriage together.

When they reached the edge of the pond, she sat down on the trunk of a huge, old cottonwood tree that had been uprooted in the Thanksgiving night storm. "So are you going to tell me where I'm supposed to wear the pearls, or do I just put them on every morning and hope I hit the right day by chance," she teased him, planting butterfly kisses on his cheeks, the end of his nose and his eyelids.

"Creole." He cleared his throat and got ready to say the words, but they wouldn't come out.

"Yes, Parker." She leaned back and really looked at him. They were just out on a comfortable evening walk. He was romantic enough that when he really popped the important question he'd choose a romantic setting. He might even be one of those types who would hide her ring in the bottom of a glass of champagne.

"I love you," he said for the first time. They knew what was in their hearts. Mere words weren't needed even from that first night four weeks ago, but it made her soul sing to hear him say the three words.

"I love you, Parker," she said.

"I even like you, Creole, and that's important," he said.

She eyed him carefully. "I like you, too, but what . . ." she said impatiently.

"I have a friend in Denton who proposed to me," he said, and a jealous surge went through her body. Surely he was not going to tell her he was going to marry another woman and she was supposed to wear the pearls to his wedding. A lonesome tear balled up on the end of her long, dark lashes, and she wiped it away.

"I told her that when I kissed the woman I intended to marry that I wanted to feel electrical shocks. I told her some other things, and she said marriages don't last more than a year in this day and age. Creole, what would you do if we were old and gray and we'd been married for sixty years, and I was dying and you were sitting beside me, holding my hand?" he asked.

"I'd cry," she said. "And I'd tell you to walk slowly because I'd be along in a little while. I couldn't live without you."

He smiled and swallowed down the lump in his throat. "Creole Hawk, will you marry me?" he said abruptly.

Her heart stopped then raced forward with a full head of steam. Her palms were clammy and every sane thought in her head vanished out into the winter wind. Her tongue stuck to the top of her mouth, and she couldn't utter a single word. She didn't know whether to listen to her heart and say "yes" or to her mother's soft southern voice and ask for some time to think about it.

"I can't marry you. Everything I love disappears." She turned her face away from him.

He gently put his hand on her cheek and brought her face back around to face him. "Billy Hawk didn't disappear. Hawk Ridge has been here since the first day of creation, and it's not going anywhere, and neither am I, Creole. I won't leave you. I might disappoint you sometimes, darling. We'll fight and we'll make up. We'll live life to the fullest. And then I'll walk slowly and wait for you when my life is finished." He looked deep into her fearful green eyes and didn't blink.

"Love is what we have, Creole," he whispered as he kissed her eyelids ever so softly. "Love is never looking back, only going forward to a future filled with each other, and love is eternal between us. Don't be afraid. Trust me."

"Yes, I will marry you, Parker," she said and peace filled her heart.

He pulled out the velvet box from his pocket and opened it to reveal a solitaire diamond set on a wide band. "One diamond for one marriage to last forever,'' he said as he picked up her hand and put the ring on her finger. ''The matching wedding band is narrow and plain, a perfect circle, just like our never ending love. I love you, Creole. You plan the wedding and set the date, but I think maybe we better get back early enough to tell those disappointed folks at the house that we're engaged.''

''It's beautiful.'' She held her hand up, catching the bright moon beams in the reflection of the glitter of the diamond. ''I love it—and I love you, Parker.''

''Oh, and the pearls? I thought you could wear them with your dress on our wedding day. Would you like the matching earrings for a wedding gift?'' He drew her even closer to him.

''Yes, I would.'' She brushed his cheek with still another kiss. ''Let's go tell Hank and Billy. I promised Mother a week's notice and that she'd only have to stay in Oklahoma for a day. I want to get married on the ranch in one week. On New Year's Eve. Is that a long enough engagement for you, Mr. Parker?''

''Six days too long,'' he laughed. ''I promised my mother a week, too. So can you plan it that quickly?''

''Trust me,'' she said brightly.

Chapter Twelve

Julia handed Creole the pearl earrings Parker gave her last night at five minutes before midnight, just before Julia turned on the porch light and motioned her inside the house. Even if it was just an old superstition that said it was bad luck for the bride and groom to see each other before the wedding, Julia wasn't taking any chances with this miracle.

"The finishing touch," she said as Creole fixed the earrings and Julia fastened the pearls around her neck. "You are a lovely bride. I'm glad you turned down your mother's offer to wear her wedding dress."

"Couldn't. It didn't make her marriage to Daddy work, and I'm not taking any chances with Parker.

I love him too much.'' She said. ''Am I ready? Where's Daddy?''

''Right here,'' he said from her bedroom door. ''Is this my daughter? Surely this isn't the girl who rounds up cattle, who runs this ranch with an iron hand and who waded through cow patties yesterday to get to that poor little freezing calf,'' he teased.

''Oh, hush,'' she snorted.

''Creole, you are beautiful. Even more so than your mother on her wedding day, and I'm a lucky man to be getting Parker for a son.'' He offered her his arm.

''You sure are,'' she smiled. ''And you don't look so shabby yourself.'' She eyed him up and down. He wore a brand-new western cut black suit, a bolo tie with a diamond clasp of the Hawk Ridge brand and new black eel boots. ''Is Parker nervous?''

''Not as much as me and Hank. Hank hasn't been a best man since I married your mother, and honey, I ain't never been a bridesmaid. Surely you'd like to change your mind and have your mother or Andrea stand beside you while the preacher says the words? It ain't too late. They both look beautiful out there.'' He nodded toward the den, which had been transformed with yards and yards of candles and flowers into a chapel for the wedding.

''Nope, you've stood beside me and fought for me all these years, so you deserve to stand up with me.'' She took his arm. ''Now, let's get this part over with. I'm ready to be Mrs. Parker Rollin.''

Parker fidgeted in front of his mother, Les and Tory and the rest of the room, which was full of close friends and relatives, as he waited for Creole to arrive on her father's arm. The preacher raised his arms for everyone to stand when Julia began playing the wedding march on the old upright piano in the foyer. Then Creole stepped into his vision and the rest of the people disappeared, as John Parker Rollin's heart crossed the room and united permanently with Creole Hawk's.

She wore a simple straight satin wedding dress with a scoop neckline and long, fitted sleeves. His pearls lay against her beautiful white skin, marking her forever as his. The side slit in her gown showed off a pair of kid leather lace-up boots as she covered the distance separating them. She wore her hair down in a cascade of loose curls, and a new white cowboy hat was perched at a jaunty angle on her head. The band was caught up in a bow at the back with long streamers flowing down her back. She carried a bouquet of a dozen white roses in a bed of feathery fern and tied with a wide satin ribbon. The smile she had on her face was only for Parker.

"Dearly beloved, we are gathered here in this home before God and these witnesses to unite John Parker Rollin and Amanda Creole Hawk in matrimony," the preacher began the ceremony. But words were just words, and vows, although sacred, were just vows. What was joined in the middle of the ranch house on Hawk Ridge that afternoon at two o'clock was the halves to two hearts, each requiring the other to make it a whole.

"Who gives this woman to be married to this man?"

"Her family and I do." Billy kissed her on the cheek and put her hand in Parker's, who felt that old familiar shock at just touching her hand.

"You may be seated," the preacher said. "The book of Ruth in the Bible has a beautiful scene," he said. "Ruth said to her mother-in-law the same thing a new bride should say to her husband, 'Intreat me not to leave thee for where thou goest, I will go, thy people shall be my people, thy gods my gods.' That's the kind of commitment I want to ask Parker and Creole to make this day. Parker, will you take this woman to be your lawfully wedded wife?"

Creole looked up into those misty gray eyes and saw a lifetime of happiness looking back at her. "I take you, Amanda Creole Hawk, to be my wife. I promise to love you, to respect you and our love, and to walk through the journey of this life with you beside me forever. And to live my life so that you can trust me until my dying day.''

''And do you, Amanda Creole Hawk, take this man to be your lawfully wedded husband?'' the preacher asked.

''I do, sir.'' Her eyes never left Parker's. ''I will be your wife. I will stand beside you in adversity and prosperity and I will respect you, love you and protect our marriage with all that I have and am. I will walk beside you through the journey of this life, and I promise to not only trust you but be trustworthy until we stand together before God in eternity, because I love you, Parker Rollin.''

The ceremony proceeded traditionally, up to and including a long kiss and a few sniffles from the two mothers behind the bride and groom.

The reception was a lavish affair with all of Allen and half the surrounding areas invited. It was held on the main street of Allen in the Senior Citizens' Building. Evangelina and Martha were disappointed when neither Parker nor Creole would consent to at least having it at a hotel in Ada. But the couple wouldn't budge, so the two mothers did what they could, decorating the room and the dance floor for a wedding reception.

Parker fed her a piece of the four-layer wedding cake and toasted their marriage with a crystal glass of some kind of sweet punch, while the photographer took pictures for all future generations to look at in the big, white satin-covered wedding book.

Then Creole took Parker by the hand and nodded toward her mother, who had stepped up to the microphone, where the band had set up for business. "Creole asked for only one favor from me at this wedding. It seemed a bit strange, but how can a mother refuse her daughter," she said, captivating everyone there with her soft southern voice as well as her beauty. "So here's my gift, my daughter," she said, and nodded to the piano player and the drummer.

Creole set her glass down and took Parker by the hand, led him to the middle of the dance floor. "Dance with me," she whispered, taking off her hat and handing it to him so she could lay her face next to his chest and listen to his heartbeat. He took her left hand in his, and she wrapped one arm around his neck and the other around his waist. He held her hat at the small of her back and drew her closer to him. Evidently her mother was about to sing something, and they were supposed to dance the first dance.

Evangelina began singing the old Cajun love ballad Creole sang to him that hot summer day out beside the pond when she asked him to dance with her. He had to swallow hard to get that silly basketball-sized lump to leave his throat. "I love you so much, Lady Creole," he whispered softly into her ear.

"And I love you, Mr. Parker," she whispered back.

"Martha?" Les said, holding out his hand and Evangelina stopped singing and the band invited everyone else onto the dance floor to join the bride and groom, who were still cuddled up waiting for the next song.

Martha nodded. Creole wasn't that spoiled child any longer, and she was delighted to have her for a daughter-in-law. Who would have ever thought she'd have a reception in the middle of Allen and would look at Parker with such love that it brought tears to his mother's eyes?

In the middle of the song Hank tapped Les on the shoulder. "Mind if I cut in?" he asked respectfully. Les smiled and nodded. Today was a time for healing old wounds, and he was wise enough to know that Martha was his wife now, and Hank was just a part of her past.

"Lovely wedding," Hank said to the short woman whom he hadn't seen in eighteen years.

"Who would have ever thought those two would end up together, with the way they used to fight."

"Or the way we'd end up apart with the way we used to love," she said right back. "Life doesn't come with guarantees, does it, Hank? You ever going to remarry?"

"Nope." He shook his head. "I married you. Loved you with my whole heart and it didn't work. I think I'll just be a grandpa soon as those two can make me one. Maybe I'll love the babies as much as I loved you. Like you say, life doesn't come with guarantees. I just thought Parker would like to see us bury any old hurts on his wedding day."

"Good idea." She nodded. The song ended. "I hated to see him come back to the ranch I hated so much, but now I'm glad he's on Hawk Ridge. He loves it. Just don't you spoil my grandbabies too much, Hank Rollin," she smiled.

"Wouldn't dream of it, ma'am." He tipped an imaginary hat toward her.

"Billy?" Evangelina was at his elbow. "I think this dance belongs to us. If Hank and Martha can bury the hatchet, surely we can."

"Probably not, but I'll dance with you," he said. "Indians hold grudges forever, you know. They're almost as bad as Cajuns."

"Worse," she said as she propped her arm on his shoulder. "I didn't want her to marry the hired hand's son, you know. But he's a nice man. I'll never forgive you for keeping her on that ranch and making her learn to love it.''

''I really don't care,'' he said flatly. ''Indians make their children love the land and their heritage. You got what you wanted when you left, Evangelina. I got the best part of our marriage. I got Creole, and now I'm getting the cream of the crop with Parker. I get to grow old watching the grandchildren grow up.''

''You still love me, you old skunk,'' she giggled.

''I always will, but that don't mean you can ever come back, you know,'' he said. ''You weren't made for Hawk Ridge. But Creole was.''

''Will you let me play with those grandchildren, too?''

''Sure, but not two weeks every summer and never on Christmas, unless you come to Oklahoma.'' He led her back to her tall, blond husband and put her hand in his. ''I'm glad you both could come to the wedding. It means a lot to the kids.''

Parker took Creole by the hand, and the two of them ran through a shower of birdseed toward his truck, which had ''Just Married'' written in white shoe polish on the back window, balloons tied to every available loop around the bed of the truck, and a hundred tin cans and one cowboy boot tied to the back.

He picked his bride up and put her in the truck on the passenger's side, then ran around to get into his side where Hank and Billy waited. Billy shook his hand one more time and crawled inside to give Creole one more hug. Hank patted his son on the back, and told him the contractors were arriving on Monday to start their new home on the back side of the ranch, so he'd better not extend the honeymoon past the weekend.

They drove to Oklahoma City where they had reservations at a hotel, and he carried her over the threshold into a plush room. He set her down, kicked the door shut with the back of his boot heel, and took her in his arms for a long, passionate kiss.

''I do love you, Creole Rollin.'' He liked the way her new name rolled off his tongue. ''And I'm glad we didn't have a six-month engagement.''

''Me, too. Six days was almost too long.'' She laughed. ''Tell me one more time just what love is—you know, like you said out there on that old cottonwood tree last week.''

''Love is . . . you,'' he said simply as he kissed her again, sealing their love, their fate and their lives together as one, forever.